Acknowledgments

A lot goes into writing a novel—even one as short as *Unlikeliest Witness*. For sure, I didn't just flap my wings by myself. Others helped make this book possible.

Without the steadfast patience, understanding and support of my family, I'd have never completed this project. Patsy, my wife, was there with me, while I was in my so-called "writing zone," practically oblivious to anything happening around me. She put up with my numerous pleas to "just give me a few more minutes to write this. I'm almost done." And she understood when I worked beyond those few minutes. A lot of stuff around the house didn't get done, and even if it did I should have done better. Tough putting up with a writer. Not just anyone will do it.

Editor Judith Geary gently and smartly made me a better writer. Judy has a keen eye for detail, consistency, authenticity and believability. Even when she lost her long-time beloved husband John to cancer, near the end of this writing project, she didn't abandon her work with me. She's the consummate professional.

My writing friend Michael Manuel read the final manuscript and made valuable suggestion. I also owe a debt of gratitude to all those colorful, unforgettable characters I have come to know while living in the mountains of East Tennessee. Vestiges of many of them are in *Unlikeliest Witness.*

I can't put a price on what I learned about the press from those I worked with and for during my short but unforgettable tenure as a professional journalist in Kentucky and Illinois. Many instances from that experience, as well as some of the fascinating nuances of small town journalism, have been woven into this novel.

They say working in journalism is like being a fighter pilot. You can only do it for so long. But even if you do it for a little while, you're bound to come away with a storehouse of information and insights for a novel. A lot of that is what I drew on for this book.

Unlikeliest Witness

Other Publications by:

Larry C. Timbs, Jr

Historical Fiction, with Michael Manuel

Fish Springs

Justice for Toby

Unlikeliest Witness

An Appalachian Novel of Suspense by

Larry C. Timbs, Jr

Larry C. Timbs Jr.
Doggy Dog Press
106 Broad St., Number 183
Elizabethton, TN 37643

Larrytimbs@gmail.com

All people, places, events and situations depicted in this novel are products of the author's imagination or are treated in a fictitious way. Resemblance to persons living or dead is incidental.

The cover image is a composite including images
from Darija Provic
https://darija91.deviantart.com/
and the
Carter County Tennessee Sheriff's Department
book design by
Luci Mott

ISBN-13: 978-1719314251

ISBN-10: 171931425X

Unlikeliest Witness

Chapter 1
A Day in the Life of the High Sheriff

Sheriff Ethan Coffman grinned as he surveyed the field before him—what appeared to be about five acres of six to seven-foot tall marijuana plants. They were lush, green and leafy. They seemed to be thriving. The high sheriff and his astounded deputy got out of the truck and took it all in.

"Well, I'll be a son of a gun!" said Deputy Bernard Bunson, rubbing the sore top of his head. "Who'da thunk it?"

"Believe it," the sheriff said. "I'd say we have several hundred plants here. And, from the looks of it, this is a primitive field—no wires, no generators, no pumps connected to a water source. But this definitely isn't wild cannabis. Somebody set these plants out, tended to them, sprayed and fed 'em, I'd say, and hoped for a big payday."

Coffman pointed to an old empty can of Mountain Dew—the drink of choice in the southern Appalachians—lying there in the weeds. Next to it was a crumpled pack of Winston cigarettes. "But guess what? There'll never be a harvest here."

About that time, the radio in the mud-covered Ford-150 Police Interceptor blared: "Taylor County One, Taylor County One, come in."

"Taylor County One here," the sheriff answered. "What is it, Mattie?"

"Got a call from the medical center, sir. Family of severely injured woman requests your presence. Says you're a personal friend of theirs. It's the Haynes family."

"Shirley Haynes?" Sheriff Coffman was a friend to most of the families in his county, and that meant he often had to deal with tragedies in families he knew well.

"Hazel Eula, I believe, the caller said."

The grandmother of the family then, the sheriff thought.

"On my way, Taylor County One."

"What now, Sheriff?" Deputy Bunsen waved a hand at the field.

"It'll all be bush hogged and burned, except for about 30 plants. Those'll be for the lab boys.

"Whoever set these plants out knew what they were doing. They couldn't have picked a more densely wooded, remote area to grow their crop. Hard to find. Hard to get to. Even hard to see from the sky, but all it took was technology and one eagle-eyed TBI agent.

"And don't go tellin' me, Bernard, that you want to be downwind when we burn all this stuff," said the sheriff, grinning.

"No sir. No sir-ee. I ain't wantin' to breathe no pot, sheriff. But who we gonna' charge?"

The sheriff told him they'd easily be able to locate the landowner but chances are that person would deny any knowledge of the cannabis. And so, the sheriff predicted, no arrests would ever be made. Thus no one would likely be charged with growing this cannabis, a felony offense in Tennessee punishable with a steep fine and prison.

"Seems like a shame, Sheriff."

"How so, Bernard?"

The deputy rubbed his sweaty brow. "All this hard work and blood, sweat and tears growin' this cash crop—and all of it up in smoke. While they's so many hungry and needy people in this ole world could use that money. And I've heerd' tell that this here marijuana can help ease the sufferin' of dyin' folks."

The sheriff listened politely and then reminded him that they both were sworn to uphold the law. What he DIDN'T reveal was that he himself had occasionally smoked the so-called wicked weed during his combat infantry days in Afghanistan and *it wasn't half bad.*

"That's what we get paid to do, Deputy. So if you want to grow and harvest and sell cannabis, consider moving to California or Colorado. But it's not allowed in Tennessee."

"Yes sir. But I was just thinkin'."

"Don't think, Bernard!" the sheriff snapped at him. "Just do your job. Let's go!"

The high sheriff and his deputy jumped back into the giant, rugged off-the-road vehicle, and Bernard put the pedal to the metal—at least inasmuch as you could do that traversing a road full of rocks, roots and ruts.

"Where we goin', Sheriff?"

"Hightail it to the medical center. There's a woman there on her death bed, and I personally know her family."

"Ten-four, Sheriff."

Their insides took a beating as the big truck, diesel fumes belching from its exhaust, lurched through the forest. They literally held on to their hats and tried to keep their heads from banging against the ceiling of their vehicle—a monster truck that clawed and groaned its way over roots, rocks, ditches, rotten mossy stumps and dead tree limbs.

They were smack dab in a part of the county known as bear and wild boar country. The latter being a rarely seen up to 400-pound animal, that, if provoked, easily became aggressive and attacked with a vengeance. But it seemed like they got clear of the wilderness in half the time it took them to get into it.

In no time they were passing Summer's Rest High School, where for fun on Friday nights locals turned out in force to support the community's pride and joy high school football team. Sheriff Coffmann, a proud graduate of the school, was one of hundreds of devoted fans who took pride in the school's gleaming new stadium—made possible by help from a star NFL player who had graduated from there. It had been named after the biggest bank in town.

"It sure is a right purty stadium, ain't it, Sheriff?" Bernard said as he slowed down in front of the athletic facility that came alive with lights and action on Friday nights.

"Just drive, Deputy, and step on it!" the sheriff commanded.

The truck lunged forward as the deputy stepped back on the accelerator.

And within seconds they had gone from the beautiful to the ugly—the latter being an unsightly, decaying textile plant with a tall smokestack, hundreds of broken windows and drab, discolored concrete walls.

"The eyesore of our little community," the deputy complained as he made a sharp left turn away from what many agreed was a thorn in the town's side. He gripped the steering wheel a bit tighter and frowned. "Why the hell don't they just implode that old ugly factory?"

"You tell me," the sheriff replied, irritated that his easily distracted driver kept taking his eyes off the road. "Now, just get on outta here and let's get to where we're goin'!"

"Sure thing, boss. I was just wonderin'... It ain't that it's just a damn ugly sight. So many of our people slaved there all their lives, and now they ain't got nothin' to show for it except that they plumb ruined their backs, wrists, ankles and necks from all that liftin' and sewin'. Or they cain't hardly breathe, with that fiber in their lungs. All that while the fat cat factory owners is retired and livin' the good life—down on some island drinkin' and dancin' and playin' golf. Don't hardly seem fair."

Ten minutes later, they pulled to the front entrance of the huge medical center in a town about 15 miles away from Summer's Rest. It was a drab, gray building that many an area resident ended up dying in. Yes, Summer's Rest had its own community hospital. But for people on life support or near taking their last breath, the medical center was where they were taken.

The high sheriff instructed his deputy to park their vehicle, hopped out and walked brisky through the front entrance revolving doors. He had been told, en route, that the Hazel Eula Haynes family would be anxiously waiting for him in the ICU waiting room.

And sure enough, they were there when he arrived. Fretting. Angry. Miserable. Crying. Desperate. Hugging. Praying. But more than anything else, helpless. Helpless to lessen the pain and suffering of Hazel Eula Haynes—their mother, grandmother and great grandmother.

Shirley, Mrs. Haynes' tearful youngest daughter, thanked the sheriff for coming, hugged him and whispered to him that she didn't think her mom would make it. Then she asked him to go with her to her mom's room—1256 in ICU.

"We've known each other for a long time, Shirley," Coffmann said, walking down the hall. "And you know you can tell me anything. I don't want you to hold anything back—no matter how bad it is."

"Ain't no words can describe this to you. You'll see for yourself soon enough," she said.

And sure enough, words couldn't have adequately captured the ghastly scene confronting the sheriff when they entered the ICU room. There, on a bed was a severely beaten 90-year-old Hazel Eula Haynes. She lay still—her blackened eyes shut and her face almost unrecognizable but her heart still beating.

An IV and other tubes were connected to her body. Monitors beeped and flashed intermittently. A nurse stayed close by her side. Occasionally the nurse would get up, take a few steps to the far side of the room and key something into a computer. But she was ever attendant to her barely hanging-on patient.

The sheriff squeezed her frail, bony claw of a hand and stroked her matted hair.

He leaned over her bed and spoke softly to her—not so much as a law enforcement officer but as a gentle, reassuring protector. "Tell me who did this to you, Miz Hazel."

Just the slightest response from the barely-alive woman lying there on the bed. She might have nodded her head.

Only her daughter Shirley had heard what the sheriff said before he turned to leave. She thanked him again for coming and embraced him.

It brought back sweet memories—all those years ago as a high school sophomore. Sharing a banana split at the Dairy Queen and then, driving, with his arm around her, to Romance Lane. Making out. Smudged lipstick. Sweaty bodies. Steamy windows and rock'n roll music blaring from the radio on his dad's 1980 hot red muscle Mustang. "Roman hands and Russian fingers," Coffmann remembered her saying with a smile. And then another sentence came back to him, eliciting a chuckle, even now after all these years. "You're the first boy I ever let touch my knees."

So long ago, the sheriff thought, *but yet in some ways just like yesterday.* And now this. Their paths crossing in this place of sickness, injury and dying in the worst way imaginable.

"Can you tell me anything about what happened to her?"

Shirley led him around a corner from her mother's room into the adjacent hallway. "I called her at eight o'clock last night like I always do to check on her. I offered to come stay with her, but she said she was fine and she'd see me the next day when I picked her up for Bible study.

"When I got there this morning, the door was broken and standing open and her trailer home had been turned inside out."

"Oh, my God, Mama!" Shirley had wailed upon finding her beloved, frail mother naked, barely conscious but still writhing and swinging her fists—as if she were trying to fight off her attacker. She lay there on an old, worn out yellow mattress with no bedding. Whoever attacked her had taken the sheets, blankets and bedspread.

Shirley had grabbed a knitted throw off the bedroom chair and wrapped her mother, hugging her close.

The old woman's face was a ruin. Her nose and eyes had been blackened. Her face was swollen, disfigured. Her neck was black and blue from someone trying to strangle her. Her arms had been beaten severely.

Her false teeth had been broken in the attack, and a piece was forced to the back side of her mouth, close to being jammed down her throat.

"I held her and rocked her and asked her who did this to her, but she couldn't tell me," said Shirley, her voice beginning to trail off. "Then I called 911. I'm sorry I don't know more."

"We'll find him." Coffmann patted her hand and answered a summons from a nurse across the hall.

"Sheriff, there's a man on the second floor that wants to see you," the head nurse of ICU said. "Says you and him go way back. He's in a pretty bad way."

Coffmann couldn't figure how a patient on another floor of such a huge medical facility had learned he was there. He had barged into the hospital lobby in muddy, grimy clothes, the only hint of his office the sheriff's star on his ball cap. Nevertheless, word traveled quickly when the high sheriff of Taylor County, Tennessee, went anywhere. He was big and rugged, with a Herculean upper torso and broad shoulders. And people recognized him, even in bordering counties, from his face on the six o'clock TV crime news.

An elevator trip and short walk down a hall later, he was in the man's room.

It was none other than Delmar Greer, who'd been in and out of the Taylor County jail at least a dozen times—mostly for petty crimes like vagrancy, trespassing and public drunkenness.

And yes, the nurse had been right. Delmar was in bad shape—very bad shape.

Like Hazel Eula Haynes, he was connected to an IV and oxygen. His face was sunken and pale. One of this front teeth was missing. The other one was black. A scraggly beard covered his wrinkled chin. His neck was tattooed. Sticking out from the bottom of a bed sheet were two swollen, purplish-veined feet.

But Delmar Greer lit up with a smile when High Sheriff Ethan Coffmann approached his bedside. "I knowed you'd come, Sheriff. That's cause you'n me's brothers. We're warriors. We fought them ragheads hard in the desert."

"That was years ago, Delmar," the sheriff replied. "The war's long over. What I'd like to know is what you're doin' in here in the hospital? Why'd they admit you?"

"Help me, Sheriff! I needa' smoke. Just one, man!" the man, practically a skeleton, pleaded. "Doc says they ain't nothin' he can do fer me." He coughed, as if gasping for air, between his sentences.

Coffmann reminded his fellow veteran that he was on oxygen and was the last person in the world who needed a cigarette. "Besides," he said, "I don't smoke. Never have. Never will."

"Get me a cigarette now, Sheriff," the man in the hospital bed pleaded. "You're the high sheriff! You can get me anything you want."

"Won't get you a cigarette, Delmar, but I'll do what I can with social services. They won't keep you in here long and my guess is that when you leave you won't have a warm place to lay your head."

More than once, the sheriff or one of his deputies had run up on the penniless, borderline mentally ill veteran sleeping amid cardboard boxes and raggedy blankets on a side street of Summer's Rest. Most recently, they'd found Delmar holding one of those scribbled signs that read "HOMELESS VETERAN, HUNGRY, BROKE. GOD BLESS."

So rather than let his fellow veteran spend a cold night on a sidewalk or in an alley or maybe even in a dumpster, Sheriff Coffmann had arrested him for vagrancy and taken him, uncuffed, to jail.

He said a few parting words of encouragement to the man whom the sheriff had saved more than once. Then he thanked the nurse for summoning him and taking care of this hurting veteran.

"We think he's about worn his welcome out at the VA, Sheriff," the nurse said. She charted how much fluid was in her patient's urinal, then emptied it down the toilet. "He's been in and out of there so many times that they think he's just wanting a place to stay, some good food, a pair of pajamas and TV. As if the VA was some kinda' hotel."

"He's got severe PTSD, ma'am," the sheriff said. "Plus, because of his addiction to opioids, he's lost everything he ever had—his family, his home, all his money, even his dog. But he was a genuine hero in Afghanistan, putting his life on the line more than once for me and others."

It made the sheriff's blood boil every time he thought of the "pill mill" certain medical doctors kept in operation. Yes, the state of Tennessee, along with the feds, had begun cracking down on physicians who overprescribed opioids like oxycodone and fentanyl. Such rogue docs faced steep fines, loss of their medical license and even imprisonment.

But the doctor who'd been treating Delmar Greer somehow had stayed under the radar, overprescribing almost every opioid in the book. Up to now, no prosecutor or drug enforcement agency had gone after him—maybe because there were much bigger fish to fry in the state's major metro areas like Knoxville, Memphis and Nashville.

The other side of the story, of course, was that without pain medications some people simply couldn't function. An example being the combat-injured and long suffering man in this hospital bed, who even today, decades after his last deployment, struggled mightily with the ugly consequences of coming ever so close to stepping on an Improvised Explosive Device (IED). But for his war dog Lucy, a German shepherd paving the way a few steps ahead of him, Delmar would have died. The bomb-sniffing canine had not detected the explosive and had taken the brunt of the blast that fateful day in Helmand province in Afghanistan. And if not for the dog's missteps, then-Sgt. Ethan Coffmann, who'd been right behind his fellow soldier, would have also died or been severely injured. Aside from the explosion, there'd been a fierce firefight, with three Americans killed and two others, including Delmar, critically wounded.

Lucy lived, but with injuries to her lungs and other internal organs. Awarded a Purple Heart, it had still taken almost an act of Congress to get Lucy transported from the veterinary hospital in Germany to the United States, where Delmar and the canine were finally reunited. But with help from the governor of Tennessee, it had happened. Man and dog would become inseparable partners for the rest of their lives. At least that was Delmar's hope.

However, Lucy's wounds got the best of her and she soon died, leaving her depressed, lonely owner to fend for himself in what seemed to him to be a cold, uncaring world. Years ago, his wife had left him for another man. But with Lucy, he'd managed to keep on keeping on. A best friend he'd have for a long time, he wishfully thought. It hadn't worked out that way. He'd been alone and in a dark place now for many years.

Poor guy, Coffmann thought. *That dog was the one living thing in the whole world that ever really cared about him and that would never abandon him. Gave it all up for his country and what'd it get him? A few medals for heroism in combat. But where is he today? Homeless, alone, addicted and in pain. Pain he can hardly stand day in and day out. Always jumpy, fidgety, nervous, sickly, depressed. That damn blast ruined him.*

Back upstairs at the sprawling medical center, devastated family members of Hazel Eula Haynes—including the daughter who found her the morning after the bloody, vicious assault—kept a round-the-clock vigil, either at her bedside or in the ICU waiting room.

"She might die," her son-in-law said. Hanging his head, so as to avoid eye contact with the family, he said it matter-of-factly as if he were talking about the weather.

"She's a fighter," his wife Shirley countered. She dabbed at her tears. "She won't give up."

"I pray that if she does die, she'll go straight to Heaven and not remember a thing about who done this evil thing to her," a long-faced grandson said. A silver cross necklace dangled about midway down his t-shirt. He was huddled somberly with the others in the waiting room.

A friend of the family angrily declared, "There surely IS evil in this world. I hope ta God they catch that SOB and throw 'em in the slammer and keep 'em there till he rots!"

"This is just one of them things," a granddaughter offered. The bright-eyed strong-in-her-faith Becky Johnson had been close to her granny all her life, having been practically raised by her when her parents had been separated. "We've all just gotta' keep prayin' and hopin' that the Lord'll not take her. But nobody should take a beatin' like that."

Wayne Ellis was a friend there with the badly shaken family. His voice quavering, he asked: "So what the devil's the PO-lice doin' 'bout all this? When they gonna' arrest somebidy?"

Hugging him, Shirley said, "The sheriff's done been here. He tried to talk to my mom but she ain't able to say nothin'. And they ain't got nary a clue who done this to her."

"Was you in there when that sheriff man spoke ta her?" he asked. "Whad'd he say ta her?"

"He asked her if she'd been beaten up and she nodded she had," Shirley said. "And when he asked her if she'd been raped, she nodded yes ta that, too."

"What I cain't figure is why Hazel?" Wayne responded. He gritted his teeth and clinched his fists. "Why'd they target her? She didn't have no money. She lived in a little run-down trailer, for God's sake! She drove a 25-year-old car. And she's 90 years old. Don't make a damned bit'a sense to me."

As the family commiserated in the waiting room, Hazel Eula Hayes—a mother, grandmother and great grandmother—hung on. Electronic instruments attached to her body monitored her heartbeat, blood pressure and oxygen levels. To help the severely beaten woman breathe, oxygen was pumped into her lungs via a tube injected into her trachea. Nutrition was pumped directly into her stomach and hydration into her bloodstream via more tubes.

Tricia May, another granddaughter, clasped her aunt Shirley's hands. She struggled to find her words, finally coming up with: "There's always hope, no matter how small. Jesus saves."

But Hazel's son-in-law wasn't convinced. "You sayin' Jesus'll come down today from them big white puffy clouds, ridin' a big white horse, and lay his healin' hands on granny? Where the devil was he the other night in her trailer? Why'd he let somethin' as God-awful terrible as this ta happen?"

Tricia stood her ground: "Psalms says the Lord is near to the broken hearted and saves the crushed in spirit.

"And did you know Granny Hazel's favorite hymn was 'Trust and Obey'? That's what we all have ta do now. Trust in Jesus."

A few more days in the ICU, however, saw no improvement in the severely beaten woman's condition. Police investigators couldn't get her to speak. So all they knew was from those slight head nods she'd given them earlier.

Her daughters and granddaughters prayed and wept by her bedside and squeezed her hands. Other kinfolk tried their best to reassure those closest to granny that she'd pull through. Some visitors knelt to the floor, closed their eyes and prayed fervently that the Lord would spare her.

No response from granny.

Doctors adjusted the IV drop, putting even stronger life-saving medicine in it.

But the critically injured woman, her breathing on the decline, worsened. Her heart grew weaker. Her blood pressure dropped. She lost what little color she had left. She was but a shadow of her old self—lying there like some sort of ancient, pallid rag doll.

Finally, the day after hospice was called in and the doctors disconnected her from all artificial life support—nutrition, hydration, oxygen—Hazel Eula Haynes stopped breathing. Her family—exhausted, prayed out and numb—was grateful that she was not forced to suffer further.

She was pronounced dead at 2 a.m., Aug. 20, 2017—10 days after being severely beaten and raped.

Tears were shed and heads hung low but after so much fretting and hoping and praying, the family also felt a sense of relief.

A hospice chaplain, who had gathered the family in a circle and directed them to hold hands, tried to console: "She's not hurtin' no more. And she's got no more heartache, ′cause we all know she's in the arms of angels.

"And remember, all of you, Judgment Day is coming. There will be an accounting, and the person who hurt Granny and took her life will be thrown into a lake of fire."

Chapter 2
A Stunned Community

Granny Hazel Eula Haynes had been viciously violated and murdered, and now she had been laid to rest and had met her maker. But for many in her home community of Summer's Rest, Tennessee, population about 12,000 in Taylor County, she would never be forgotten. For one thing, a woman who had spread kindness and goodness throughout her life had been the helpless, innocent victim of an unspeakable crime—a cruel act committed by some kind of monster who had total disrespect for any semblance of humanity, let alone an iota of feeling for a loving, old, church-going lady.

"In my 30 years in law enforcement in the state of Tennessee, I've never seen anything as abominable as this," a forensics investigator had declared. The report from the state medical examiner, based primarily on the medical reports from her admission to the hospital, concluded that Hazel Eula Haynes had died from severe, forced blunt trauma to her head and neck and to some of her internal organs. Hemorrhaging had occurred in her nasal and eye areas, and her chest and abdomen had absorbed multiple strikes—perhaps with a hammer or some other pointed tool. In addition, whoever attacked her had bruised her arms, as if he'd punched them as she tried to fight him.

The report also concluded that Miz Hazel, as many of her friends called her, had been sexually assaulted—with swabs of blood (but no semen) taken from her vagina and buttocks. There was evidence of penetrating rectal trauma. The medical examiner noted that Miz Hazel's assailant had undoubtedly used a condom, but he had nevertheless bloodied her genitalia with his roughness.

The cause of death was ruled unquestionably as a homicide.

After her body was released by the medical examiner, Miz Hazel's family quickly arranged for her funeral.

Because the horrific death had sent shock waves throughout the small mountain community, it took three hours for everyone in the receiving line to pay their respects—and offer their support and prayers—for the family. Many in line blew a kiss to Miz Hazel's flower draped closed casket when they walked by it. A thick spray of white roses formed the centerpiece, while potted plants of reds, yellows and purples framed each side of the casket.

Hugs, tears and condolences, and anger at such an abominable crime, filled the little chapel.

The Rev. Robert S. Hamilton of the deceased's home church delivered the eulogy. A thin impeccably dressed slender man with spit-shined black shoes, he straightened his tie as he approached the platform in back of the brass-handled pungent cedar casket.

"Pretty, ain't it, if they is such a thing," one of Miz Hazel's kin whispered.

The preacher opened his well-worn Bible, took a deep breath and began. "Brothers and sisters, we are all here today to say goodbye to one of the kindest, sweetest, most humble women I have ever had the honor of knowing.

"To say that Hazel Eula Haynes lived a virtuous, selfless Christian life is the understatement of the century," the middle-aged pastor continued. "Because everyone who knew her or who knew of her can attest that she was the very best of us.

"Mother, grandmother, great-grandmother, foster parent to children who had been abandoned or abused, hospital volunteer, worker at the homeless shelter and soup kitchen, devoted member of her Sunday School class, a woman who even let others borrow her car—her only car—if they needed a way to get to the grocery store or to the doctor, a person who opened her pocketbook at a restaurant and bought food for a hungry stranger, a woman who never stopped reading her Bible and tried her best every day to live the Good Book.

"And the list of good deeds of kindness, sweetness and gentleness goes on and on, folks. Because Hazel Eula Haynes was the best of us.

"She didn't ask for much, and she loved the simple, basic things in life—a good cup of coffee, family picnics, a grandbaby bouncing on her knees, knitting, sharing meals at her favorite restaurants—McDonald's, the Waffle House and Susie's Kitchen—with her close friends and family, and sometimes even with a complete stranger if they looked destitute and hungry.

"And now her gentle and quiet spirit has been taken away from us. She was hurt badly, and she was violated, and she never recovered from whoever attacked her so viciously. Never even could say goodbye to her loved ones! Couldn't touch or kiss them one last time.

"And yes, we are all angry and sorrowful and puzzled—and many of us are raging with bitterness—at how someone so EVIL could take our precious, sweet Miz Hazel from us. Rest assured, the doer of this dispicable deed will pay for this crime—if not in this life, then in eternity."

"May he rot in Hell!" an old, bearded, toothless man in overalls yelled from a pew about midway back in the crowded chapel.

Her hair pulled back in a tight bun, a porky woman dressed in black in a pew just a few steps away from the casket agreed: "Yep! But I'd like the bastard to be castrated first!"

Heads nodded, bodies shuffled, some people shook their fists and an uneasy murmur filled the packed, increasingly-tense sanctuary.

The nervous pastor raised his hands and tried to regain control, assuring his listeners that the Lord would render righteous indignation against anyone so wicked as to harm a saintly woman like Miz Hazel. "The Good Book says He will demand a reckoning from anyone who hurts a widow or orphan or other vulnerable human being," the pastor reminded them. "Yes, we can feel angry, betrayed and crushed by what happened to one of our sisters in Christ, but we need not despair. The Bible tells us that Hazel Eula Haynes triumphed in this life. That's because she gave her life to Christ at an early age and then she trusted in God and followed God the rest of her days."

"Then why'd He let her get murdered and raped?!" a tall, gawky man blurted out. He stood up and shouted, "Lord help us all!"

A woman sitting next to him, cooling herself with a funeral home fan, said "SHUSH!"

A suit-clad gentleman to the immediate right of the belligerent yeller grabbed and pulled him back down to his seat. The snarling yeller shook him off angrily, as if to declare that he'd say what he wanted wherever he wanted to.

Beads of sweat dribbling down his forehead, Pastor Hamilton sensed things might get ugly if he held his listeners much longer. So he tried to close with an uplifting message: "Love deeply, brothers and sisters—even if it hurts to do that. Love the sinner. Love each other. Stretch your love. Live the good life. That's what Jesus wants. And that's what Hazel Eula Haynes would want you to do. That's why Miz Hazel has won—even though she died so viciously. She's in Heaven smiling down at all of us, urging us to honor her life by loving and serving others—even the worst among us."

"Bull crap!" the angry yeller spouted loud enough so that half the unsettled funeral-goers could hear him.

Chapter 3
Gossip and Guessing

Within hours of Miz Hazel's funeral, they reverently laid her to rest, amid rose petals and her favorite verses from the Bible, in a grave on a windswept hillside of Heaven's Valley Cemetery.

But the solemnity of the funeral and the peacefulness her final resting place did nothing to calm the storm that had begun brewing days before her death. Upon hearing about the crime, folks in Summer's Rest had been shocked and fearful. Now the little mountain town was abuzz with rampant speculation and gossip.

Her unseemly death was the talk of the community anywhere folks gathered—at barbershops, beauty shops and morning coffee klatches at McDonald's, Hardees and Susie's Kitchen—the latter with signs on the dining room's yellow cinderblock wall that said "FRIENDS GATHER HERE" and "THINK HAPPY THOUGHTS." Miz Hazel's untimely death also got talked about at Walmart, Tractor Supply, grocery stores, the hospital, funeral homes, on the courthouse steps, at the DMV, on sidewalk benches downtown, in church parking lots and on Facebook and Twitter.

What heartless sicko, people wondered, could have done this and when'll they catch him? Speculation was it could have been anybody, but quite a bit of the talk focused on the hundreds of brown-skinned migrant workers who toiled in the fields just outside Summer's Rest, performing backbreaking labor under the scorching sun that no white person would want to do.

"Wouldn't surprise me atall if one'a them wetback Mexicans did it," Rayburn McCloud groused at the regular morning coffee group at McDonald's. "They bring'em in here ever' year to pick ′maters on that big spread on the north enda' the county."

Between slurps of coffee, an old timer at the crowded table mused: "You meanin' at the Drinkwaters' farm?"

Turning up his nose and scowling, McCloud shot back: "Well, they mighta' come from there or from the Wetmores' strawberry crops. Cause them Mexican pickers is bein' trucked in here by the hunderds. They even give 'em places to live and 'bout a dozen of them cram into the same old doublewide. They's a whole bunch of them doublewides near where they pick—bought'n paid for by old man Wetmore.

An eavesdropping woman from a nearby table said, "Did you just say Drinkwaters and Wetmores?" She snickered between sips from her coffee cup.

"Well, that be their names, stranger!" McCloud declared angrily. "And if you be wantin' to get in with what we're talking 'bout, feel free to move your little nosy fanny over here."

"I'll stay right where I am, thank you, but I wouldn't go pointin' fingers at folks you've never even met. Them Mexicans work hard and send a right smart bunch of money back to their loved ones in Mexico. I know cause I see 'em at the Walmart bank center ever' day. They ain't bad people.

"And that ain't the halfa' it," she added intensely. "Them Mexicans happen ta' be doin' the back breakin' work that no white person'll do. You seen all them big signs down at the grocery store? The ones showing the fat cat white farmers, grinnin' like possums, holdin' the fresh fruit and vegetables they claim they growed and picked fer us. The ones that say 'Eat locally grown fruit and vegetables and reward your local farmers!'

"Well, that ain't nothin' but a bald-faced lie." She flailed her arms and grimaced. "Fact is, it's our brown-skinned brothers and sisters from Mexico that's bending or kneeling all day in the blazing hot sun. They're the ones pickin' their hands plumb raw bringin' in the strawberries, tomatoes, squash, cucumbers or whatever else it is we're buyin' from our grocery store."

Her listener shot back: "They're still fereigners takin' away our jobs!"

With that, the jeans-clad 40-ish woman scooped up her tray and moved to a table at the far end of the restaurant. Her bleached hair partially covered a tattoo on her neck and her eyeglasses dangled from a string around her neck.

But try as she might, she couldn't seem to get away from what she thought of as the small town's narrow mindedness and prejudice.

At the table next to her, for example, a brown-skinned, dark-haired young restaurant employee in an apron ventured over to the threesome and offered to refill their cups.

"You a terrorist?" one of the drinkers growled. He rared back in his chair and folded his arms. "You look like one'a them I-Rain-ians."

"Nope," she replied unflinchingly, hoisting her shoulders back. "You a member of the KKK?"

Taken aback at such a quick rebuke, the man practically coughed up his coffee.

At a booth in a far corner of the restaurant, discussion focused on the idea of a drug-crazed, murderous addict breaking into Miz Hazel's home.

"People have a lotta' pain here, and you can't get pain pills except from your grandma and she has to sell'em to you so she can pay her light bill," one woman said.

"Now how the devil you knowin' that?" her tablemate asked.

"Cause my own granny'n me's got this thing worked out. She ain't got no money and I ain't able to buy no pills. So ever' time I get my paycheck from Walmart, I help her and she helps me. But don't you go running your mouth 'bout that!"

The woman she spoke to, swallowing the last of her biscuit, swore she wouldn't reveal anything about this but warned her friend that she could be putting herself in danger.

"People are needin' money for drugs and so they're breakin' in and robbin' and stealin' and whatever they can do. So how you makin' sure nobody don't break into your own house and steal them pain pills you get from your granny?"

"That's easy," the first woman said. "I'm locked and loaded. Any fool breaks into my house, they get a bullet right quick like. I'll tell you what I do. I sit at my dining room table with my gun. And I watch my front door and my backyard. Ain't nobody gonna' set foot on my property without me knowin' 'bout it."

And so it went with the talk at busy places across town. And when the chatter wasn't about the murder of Hazel Eula Haynes, the coffee drinkers had a way of turning to just about anything under the sun, but mainly the weather, who had just died, whose spouse had left whom, what preacher had just gotten fired and who'd just gone to the nursing home. Almost always, too, the conversation had a way of reverting to their aches and pains: their rotator cuffs, kidney stones, gall bladders, knee and hip replacements, arthritis. Whether you wanted to hear about it or not, you'd also get the scoop on their medicines and doctors, their upcoming appointments and what their Medicare did and didn't pay for. All of this being their familiar tried and true topics for connection, conversation and community.

Occasionally someone would recall something comical.

"I took out an old leakin', smellin' porcelain toilet from my house," said Walter McCrory, chewing the fat with two other men at his breakfast table at McDonald's. "Had to wrassle and lift and pull that dad-blasted thing like nobidy's business. And finally got it inta' the backa' my station wagon. Hauled it ta the landfill and damned if the attendant at the gate didn't want to know what I wuz bringin' in. When I told him I had an old toilet, he grinned and asked me, 'Did you flush it before you loaded it?'"

Sidesplitting laughter from his listeners.

Still, however, the biggest recent thing on people's minds—and what they tended toward dwelling on the most—was the unsolved murder of one of their own.

At Renee's Beauty Shop, Louise Trivette and Susan Roberts each primped in front of the mirror when they paid their bill. But that didn't stop the two longtime residents of Summer's Rest from gabbing about what seemed to be consuming the whole town.

"The End Days is almost here," Louise said. As she dug into her purse for a tip to leave for Renee, she said the terrible death of Hazel Eula Haynes had angered the Lord. She predicted He would demand retribution.

Susan chimed in: "I've heard tell that God's already started ghostin' our community."

Louise raised her eyebrows as she closed her purse. "What you mean by ghostin' it?"

"I mean God's breakin' it off with this bad town. He's leavin' us to go about with whatever sin we wanta commit. He's give up on us."

"God don't give up on nobody, ever!" Louise fired back. "And if he's a ghost, He's a friendly one."

Not that the picturesque little town of Summer's Rest hadn't been shocked big time before. About 80 years earlier, one of the most infamous murder cases in the history of Tennessee had rocked the historic community to its core.

Three little girls, all of them under age 10, had been dynamited in their bed while they slept—their faces barely recognizable after the blast. Their mother, asleep in an adjoining room, had survived but suffered severe injuries.

The murders—occurring in Rabbit Foot Holler, a few miles outside of Summer's Rest—drew national attention to a mountain community that seldom got coverage beyond the county line. Reporters from New York, Boston, St. Louis and Chicago descended on Summer's Rest, wanting to know if it was true that a "mean streak" ran through the mountains of Appalachia. Journalists from afar had heard tantalizing tales of the Hatfields and McCoys, fueding families in the mountains of West Virginia and Kentucky, and so within that context they focused on Summer's Rest.

"I remember them three little caskets in a wagon bein' pulled by horses," said 95-year-old Myrtle Robinson. Holding her listeners spellbound at Renee's Beauty Shop, she told them how two of those convicted of the dynamite murders were sentenced to the electric chair.

"I ain't never seen such crowds at the courthouse," she recalled. "I was only a little girl but people was pushin' and shovin' to get into that courtroom. And you know what? One of them scoundrels never did get to the electric chair. That's causin' he hung himself by his belt in the county jail. Why, my uncle Sam somehow got a locka' his hair when he went to the jail to give haircuts. And he kept it in his private papers till the day he died. I think his widow's still got it."

Her hair in curlers and her jaws chomping on a wad of gum, Opal

Jenkins put her two cents in on the three murders that occurred so long ago: "My momma told me all about it. She said them girls was killed cause their daddy somehow got caught up in bad blood over a gamblin' debt. Them that killed his daughters was out for revenge and payback."

Martha Sue Remington, in one of the waiting chairs, was always looking for love and read all she could about how to attract a man. She peeked up from her Redbook magazine—with the big headline on the cover "Ten Ways to Drive Him Crazy in Bed"—and said, "I've seen their graves up at Powder's Mountain. And it's a cryin' shame that the weeds has almost taken over their tombstones."

But the dynamite murders, bad as they were, weren't the only gruesome crimes to rock Summer's Rest, situated about 10 miles from one of the cleanest and most beautiful TVA lakes in the South.

About 40 years before the rape/murder of Miz Hazel, an elderly church deacon had been knocked out, dragged from his house and tied up and gagged and hanged from an apple tree in his front yard. Those who hanged the widower in the community of Howardtown, five miles from Summer's Rest, apparently thought mistakenly that he had $10,000 in life insurance money salted away under his mattress.

"I knowed when we strung 'em up, it was wrong, but it was like we couldn't stop," one of the convicted young men said tearfully. "They was a crowd 'a people with us that night and they kept yellin' 'hang 'em'! And so we did and then we all drove downtown for a Mountain Dew and hamburger at Charlie's Restaurant. And we slept pretty as you please that night…"

And even more recently—just a few years prior to Miz Hazel's murder—the dismembered skeletal remains of a young woman had been found in a storage unit in Summer's Rest. Law enforcement had suspected foul play when a couple of fishermen ran upon Jackie Filbert's 1992 Ford pickup truck at Wylie Lake. The front end of the vehicle jutted out from the surface of the water.

A witness to the drug-related robbery and murder of Filbert tipped off police to check the storage unit. And there they found the unfortunate soul's partially decomposed, dismembered body. An ugly find, for sure, but not one that area residents fretted much about. That's because no one had ever heard of the woman from a nearby state, and they never could figure how she'd gotten herself killed in the first place. If anything, the unseemly remains gave some grist for the local gossip mill.

"I heared tell she was wantin' a divorce, but her husband gave her a separation instead," a mole-faced, stringy whittler allowed on the bench in front of the courthouse.

When one of this fellow whittlers laughed, another bench sitter took offense. "How'd you feel if somebody cut your blood kin all ta pieces and stuffed 'em into a Uhaul storage locker? Why, it's plumb awful what happened ta' that lady."

Between chews of his tobacco and dangling his thumbs in his dirtstained overalls, another whittler said: "It was a boogerish way somebidy kilt' her."

And so the talk went and it kept churning for weeks after Miz Hazel's funeral. The community had a history of infamous crimes, but no one said they could recall anything on the scale of evil that took the sweet granny's life. Rape and strangling and beating and murder of a 90-year-old woman who never hurt a soul in her whole life. Of a mother, grandmother and great-grandmother asleep in her trailer, most likely, after taking her bedtime medicines, reading verses from her Bible and saying her prayers.

And then an intruder. A stranger? Someone she knew or who knew her? Someone who needed money for dope? Someone who was demented or psychotic?

Did she even have the slightest inkling of what was coming? Reach for her phone? Kick and claw and punch and scream? Plead for mercy? Savaged. Violated. Murdered. Everything she had ever been, everything she was, everything she would be, all of it brutally snatched away.

Chapter 4

Attack through the Local Press

Six weeks after the murder of Hazel Eula Haynes, the Taylor County Sheriff's Department had still not made an arrest. The townspeople continued to grow more uneasy.

The unrest reached a boiling point when a group of irritated residents, calling themselves "Concerned Citizens for the Welfare and Safety of Summer's Rest," took it upon themselves to pay for a full page ad in the *News-Journal.* And they delivered it in person.

"WE DEMAND JUSTICE!" was the banner headline in large bold print at the top of the camera-ready ad they had sought to get published.

"And we want justice NOW!

"Why hasn't our Sheriff's Department found the person who took the life of one of our most precious senior citizens, Hazel Eula Haynes?

"There's a cold-blooded murderer on the loose and what does our sheriff and his deputies do?

"They're busy writing speeding tickets and arresting teenagers for neckin' on Romance Lane at night.

"Or they're drinking coffee and devouring doughnuts down at Bailey's Diner.

"We the taxpayers of Summer's Rest have had enough! Either Sheriff Ethan Coffmann should resign or he should be fired by the city council, mayor and city manager.

"If he hasn't made an arrest in the Haynes case by the end of this month, and if he hasn't been fired, we will begin circulating a petition to have him recalled from his office.

"The Sheriff better wake up and do his job!"

When they presented their ad to the *News-Journal*'s marketing manager, Marie Garland, she politely and nervously asked them to wait while she consulted her boss. She knew that *News-Journal* publisher Jake Cravens and Sheriff Ethan Coffmann were good friends. They were longtime buddies. They and their wives went out to dinner together every Friday night. They drank and played poker together at the American Legion. Both of them Afghanistan veterans, they were also regulars at the VFW.

She was also acutely aware that the always news-hungry reporters at the little newspaper regularly leaned on the county sheriff for the latest about local crime and the courts. In fact, crime and court news were staples of the paper. Readers—those older types who weren't yet into online news— eagerly looked forward to each edition of the newspaper to find out who got arrested, indicted, married, divorced, who filed for a building permit and who bought or sold property. And the sheriff usually saw to it that his deputies and courthouse officials cooperated fully with the *News-Journal*.

Publisher Cravens, whose great grandfather had founded the *News-Journal* decades earlier, wasn't happy when Ms. Garland burst into his office. He told whoever he was talking to that he'd be right back with them, cupped the phone and motioned for his marketing manager to have a seat in front of his large, polished mahogany desk.

"I'm sorry, but this is going to take a minute, sir," Ms. Garland said. She took a deep breath and wiped the sweat from her forehead. "I have a group of angry people in the front office and they're demanding …"

Before she could finish her sentence, her balding, rotund boss slammed the phone down, put out his cigar and leaned back in his big, plush, swivel office chair. "Who are they and what the hell do they want us to do?!" Cravens snapped. "If it's that Johnson couple that owns the grocery store—threatenin' us if we run the name of their oldest son, who got caught for shopliftin' last Saturday, tell 'em they're wastin' their damned time.

"If we run one person's name who's arrested for stealin', we run 'em all! Why can't people understand that?"

"I'm afraid it's not any of that, sir," said Ms. Garland, trying to keep her composure. "It's about the sheriff and the murder of Hazel Eula Haynes."

"What about it?" Cravens, sidling up closer to his desk, suddenly was a bit more subdued.

"They're not happy with the fact that the Sheriff's Department hasn't made an arrest in that case." She clutched her elbows and pursed her lips as she spoke. "I tried to tell'em we've got no control over what the sheriff or his deputies do, but they wouldn't listen. So now they're wantin' us to run a full page ad, in our next edition, attacking Sheriff Coffmann for draggin' his feet on the murder case. They want him fired if he don't arrest nobody by the end of this month."

Cravens' jaw dropped slightly as he ran his left hand down the length of his finely polished desk—which had nothing on it, save for his phone: no papers, no pens or pencils, no computer, no in-basket and no out-basket. He kept the ashtray for his Cuban cigars in the top left drawer.

He straightened his bright blue tie and brushed off unseen dust from the lapels of his jacket. He thought for a few seconds before speaking. "We don't want no trouble with the sheriff. He's a good man. He's my friend and he's done a bang-up job keeping our community safe. He's the last man in the world I want my newspaper to get crossways with. Am I clear about that, Ms. Garland?

"Besides, no way they could afford a full-page ad anyhow. That'd be over $5,000. Tell'em to be on their way and save their pennies. Or if it's burnin' a hole in their pockets, tell'em to make a donation to the Salvation Army. Now let me get back to running my newspaper. You understand?"

When she told the publisher that they had put a stack of money—all of it in hundred-dollar bills—on her desk, he was shocked. "You mean they brought that much cash with them? They have that kind of money? Tell me I just heard you wrong."

"Sir, they put crisp new bills on my desk and told me there was more where that came from."

"And did you tell'em what our policy was about slanderin' someone in the newspaper?"

When she reminded the publisher about the ad the paper ran just a few weeks ago for the KKK, he flinched. "Well, they paid cash on the barrel head and that ad was to publicize a cross burnin' up on Muldrow's Hill, Ms. Garland. They weren't exactly defaming any one person."

She reminded the newspaper owner that the KKK ad had, in fact, cast some folks in a flagrantly negative light. "Sir, that ad asserted that black people were just a cut above apes. That they were deadset on killin' off the white race. And the ad contained the N word."

"Well, this is different! Sheriff Coffmann is a duly elected official of our county. He's a war hero. He's respected and he's put many a piece of thievin' or drunken trash behind bars.

"I won't have my newspaper aidin' and abettin' a buncha' so-called do-gooders set on drivin' our respected sheriff outta office!" The publisher slammed his right palm down on his desk, bolted up from his chair and flung open his office door to usher his marketing manager out.

But she didn't move. Instead, she told her boss what the group threatened to do if the newspaper didn't publish their ad. They'd get flyers printed and have them mailed to every residence in Summer's Rest—with the notation that the town's newspaper had refused to take their money because of an unholy alliance between the publisher and sheriff.

"Well ain't that somethin'!" Cravens bristled. "Stall'em while I go pay a personal visit to the good sheriff. Tell'em we're takin' their request under advisement till we consult with our lawyers."

"What if they ask me what that means?"

"Cook somethin' up! Tell'em anything to get'em off our back for a day or two. And remind'em of our slogan: "We're the only newspaper on the planet that gives a damn about Summer's Rest and Taylor County."

Cravens grimaced as if he'd been punched in the gut. "Dammit to hell! First the KKK, and now this!"

Within a few minutes, the smartly dressed Jake Cravens was on his way to the sheriff's office in his brand new maroon Ford Thunderbird. Not wanting to have to deal personally with the irate citizens attacking his law enforcement friend, he had first exited the newspaper building through a back door.

When Cravens pulled into the combination jail/courthouse parking lot, he noticed a long line of people outside the jail entrance. He had obviously arrived just as visitation was set to begin for those in jail.

As bad as the day had begun turning out for him, it was still beautiful, with a blue sky, a few scattered whispy clouds that looked like white daffodils and a bright yellow sun.

In contrast to the nice, balmy weather were the people standing in the somber line outside the jail. They ran the gamut from the elderly to teenagers. And because the line was so long, the publisher thought it was a good bet that the jail was filled to capacity.

One of the largest and most drab buildings in Summer's Rest, the recently built $28 million combination jail/courthouse, sat curiously adjacent to a Little League baseball park. The town unquestionably needed such a sprawling jail and courthouse. Because on days that criminal court was in session, you always had a hard time finding a parking space in the jail parking lot, let alone a place to sit in the courtroom.

People got in trouble in Summer's Rest. A lot of people.

The newspaper publisher turned his nose up as he approached the sheriff's office. To him, most of those who had shown up to visit their loved ones in the sheriff's jail were hillbilly bottom feeders. In his pressed suit and shiny new shoes, he was quite a contrast to those waiting outside the jail lobby entrance.

A chunky man with stringy purplish hair and piercings in his lips and nose chatted away on his cell phone. On his shirt was the slogan: "The more I get down on her, the better she likes it."

Another man behind him looked like he hadn't shaved in a week. His camouflage cap, bearing the insignia of the Confederate flag, was pulled down to his ears and on the back of his shirt was a picture of a hunting dog and two ducks. The faded blue shirt read: "Southern By Choice!"

One 300-pound plus woman, rolls of fat jiggling under her orange UT t-shirt as she shuffled forward, had a cigarette dangling from her mouth and a snotty-nosed kid in her arms.

"Acres and acres of lumpy ass," Cravens muttered to himself.

Next to her was a boney man in a black baseball cap with the bill turned up. Big green plastic hoop earrings hung from his ears. He had his shirt tail out and wore ragged, faded jeans. Booger hairs stuck out of his nose.

"Poor excuse for a human being," Cravens groused under his breath. "Looks like he crawled out from under a rock."

Others in the line were equally downtrodden. To Cravens, they and their kin or friends—who were in jail—were roughneck hillbilly scum. Their clothes looked to have come from the Salvation Army or from the Haven of Good Deeds—which provided clothing and furniture for those down on their luck. Same with their barely held together shoes or scuffed-up boots.

And their cars and trucks parked outside the jail? Many were dented, or the paint was peeling, or at least one window was cracked, and tires were slick and worn down to the metal. A few had headlights or taillights missing or fenders or rear ends that had been smashed. Duct tape held several of the vehicles together.

A testament to the town's definite conservative underbelly, the publisher noticed plenty of NRA bumper stickers including one that proclaimed, "I'll Give You My Guns When You Pry Them From My Cold Dead Hands!" There, too, on vehicles in the jail parking lot were "Jesus Saves" stickers and Confederate flags. Other pronouncements like "Lock her up!" and "Build that wall!" adorned many a pickup truck with the proverbial gun rack in the rear window and crushed styrofoam cups, empty cigarette packs and old snuff and dented Mountain Dew cans on the dashboard.

Cravens took one last look back and sneered at all of it as he opened the door to the sheriff's office.

Chapter 5

Encounter with the High Sheriff

Pushing through the metal framed glass double doors to the sheriff's office, newspaper publisher Cravens was greeted by an officious, attractive desk clerk who screened every person wanting time with her boss. In this case, however, the curvy, who-didn't-miss-anything clerk just smiled and gave her visitor a perfunctory wave—signifying to him that the sheriff would see him immediately.

"He's not in a very good mood today, I'm afraid, Mr. Cravens," Mattie said, ushering him down a short hallway lined with pictures of waterfalls, mountains and wildlife. At the sheriff's personal office, a sign on the frosted window of the entrance read: "TAYLOR COUNTY HIGH SHERIFF'S OFFICE AND COMMAND CENTER"

Cravens thanked the clerk and said he'd take things from there.

He found an irritated and fidgety Ethan Coffmann. The chief law enforcement officer of Taylor County had always relished the title "High Sheriff," in Cravens' opinion, because he thought of himself as somehow above and beyond the ordinary Tennessee sheriff. So important that he dressed casually—in civilian clothes—while his deputies always wore starched brown uniform shirts, black pants with gold stripes down the sides, shined black shoes and had their thick black belts laden with their revolver, night stick, handcuffs and radio. On the shoulder patches of the deputies' shirts, as well as on their caps, were silver 6-point badge insignias. Gold stripes on their lower sleeves signified a deputy's rank.

Not so with Sheriff Coffmann, who preferred a polo shirt with a sports jacket, jeans or casual slacks and athletic shoes. He wore no stripes, badges, stars or medals. So in that regard, Taylor County's high sheriff figured he could easily blend in with a crowd—if he so chose—and be treated just like anyone else. And though he didn't advertise it, the high sheriff always packed heat—a Smith & Wesson .38-caliber, 2-inch barrel, cylinder-loaded revolver tucked inside the breast pocket of his jacket.

Coffmann, a former combat Marine, had been elected—and then reelected, twice, to four-year terms—by a landslide each time. For a man whose charge it was to arrest and jail so many wrong doers, he had been well thought of—until the murder of Hazel Eula Haynes. He had a reputation for running a clean, professional department and a jail that treated all inmates humanely.

His brand was a tough no-nonsense sheriff who protected and served the taxpayers of Taylor County. And though the county, like so many others in the mountains of East Tennessee, suffered from a burgeoning methamphetamine epidemic, Coffmann and his deputies had of late made a number of drug related arrests—all of them well publicized by the *News-Journal.*

Barrel chested, with piercing blue eyes, a chiseled nose, bushy eyebrows and a crewcut on a head atop a thick neck, the 6 foot, 6-inch Coffmann got up from his chair and shook hands with Cravens.

The outwardly congenial sheriff smiled and patted his publisher friend on the back, as the two of them exchanged pleasantries.

But Cravens sensed something amiss. The 240-pound fearless sheriff wouldn't look him straight in the eye, and he seemed somehow unsettled. It was as if the man pledged with "Making Taylor County a Better Place to Live, Work and Play"—that had been Coffmann's slogan throughout his three campaigns—was worried.

"Now, Ethan, you're not foolin' me one bit. What's eatin' at you?" Cravens asked. He spoke above the din of crackling radio static in the adjoining dispatcher's office.

"You know full well, Jake, I can't be goin' into police business with you. That'd be breach of my professional duty. I'm sworn to uphold the law, not to go into the nitty gritty, some of it not for public consumption, of what we're doing to keep the citizens of our county safe."

"Don't give me that mumbo-jumbo sheriff's office shit!" Cravens snapped. "And remember who helped get you elected in the first place. Don't you dare forget where you came from! Why, if it wasn't for my newspaper, you'd have—"

Before he could finish that sentence, the muscular, broad-shouldered sheriff sighed, lowered his head and mumbled, "Ok, Ok. Close the door."

Swearing his close friend to secrecy, the sheriff proceeded to share with him the broad outlines of a day that had gone from bad to worse. One of his favorite deputies had gotten caught red-handed having sex with an inmate. "He was transportin' her to state prison, Jake, and he couldn't keep his zipper up."

Cravens grinned and asked, "How'd he get caught?"

His deputy had pulled over at a rest stop, and the two of them—deputy and inmate—had hightailed it to a tree-shaded picnic table. And then they'd had at it—"like two rabbits in heat," Coffmann said.

Cravens snickered.

The problem: Picking up litter, unbeknowst to the couple, was a rest area maintenance worker with a cellphone camera. He had not only caught them in the act but also filmed the deputy's patrol car and license plate.

Result: Career over. Marriage shattered. Sheriff's Office humiliated.

"So what'll happen to him now, Ethan?"

"Well, he's being held in my slammer, on $100,000 bond, and tomorrow he'll be arraigned before Judge Robert Pendleton. And then I'm sure he'll be charged with first degree sexual offense."

"So how's he takin' all this?"

Clearing his throat and sighing, Coffmann said, "Not good at all. He's devastated. His wife wants him gone from their home. His kids'll surely get picked on at school. And soon as he's charged, I'm firing him." The sheriff gave the publisher a pleading "Can you keep this out of the newspaper?" look.

The chief executive of the press in Summer's Rest had encountered this request many times from otherwise upstanding, respected people who'd gotten themselves in serious trouble with the law.

"I can't make any promises, Ethan. If he's charged and then if he's indicted, his name will go in the paper. You know how that works. No exceptions when it comes to publishing the public record."

Sheriff Coffmann stared straight through him. "Yeah, like it was when one of my men arrested your favorite grandson for driving under the influence. And you called me at 2 a.m. after he'd been arrested and cuffed and begged me to drop the charge."

The publisher wasn't fazed. "My grandson's young. He's a good kid. Straight A student. He made a mistake—unlike your deputy who knew exactly what he was doing. And your deputy is how old?"

"Thirty-five, ten years with the sheriff's department, deacon in his church, coach of a Little League team, married with three kids."

Cravens, lowering his voice, said, "I hate it for him and his family and for you. Maybe the judge can help make this whole thing go away. And if that happens, it won't make the paper. I'll see what I can do."

Sensing all might not be lost, the sheriff patted Cravens on the back and asked if he could pour him a cup of coffee. He'd made it a point earlier to instruct his desk clerk to brew a fresh pot.

"I take it black, thanks."

"And help yourself to a piece of candy, Jake," the sheriff said, removing the lid of the glass jar full of Hershey Kisses he kept on his desk. The sheriff knew Cravens could pull strings with most anyone in the power structure in Taylor County. He rubbed shoulders with the county's richest and most well-heeled citizens. He did them favors, and they reciprocated. Because sooner or later in a small community, you do things or say things that you later regret, and you don't want them to show up in print. So it paid to stay on good terms with a man who "bought ink by the barrel," as one wealthy elite in Summer's Rest put it.

"Another thing's really botherin' me, Jake," the sheriff said as he finished pouring them both a cup of hot brew.

"Lay it on me, my old friend," Cravens responded, "but whatever it is, I can't promise I'll keep it outta my newspaper."

"No, it's nothing like that," said the sheriff. "Honcho is hurt really bad. He's at the vet's office right now in surgery. I know he's only a dog, but he's one of the best police K-9s in the country. And damned if a no-good, worthless meth addict didn't beat him in the head with a baseball bat!"

Honcho, a 75-pound sable German shepherd, had been a valued

asset of the sheriff's department. Working side by side with his handlers, Honcho had sniffed out many an explosive or illicit drug. He had found missing persons in some of the thickest, most rugged, snake-infested terrain in East Tennessee. And he had tracked down on-the-run, on-foot criminals like nobody's business.

A sympathetic Cravens asked, "So what happens now? Will the dog pull through?"

When Coffmann said the entire sheriff's department was praying for Honcho, the publisher nodded knowingly and added that he hoped the scoundrel who hurt Honcho would get his comeuppance.

"The son-of-a-bitch'll be charged with assault on a police officer, and you can print that in big type on the front page," the sheriff said. "Put his ugly mugshot right next to Honcho's picture so that everybody around here knows that one of this department's best is a K-9 that's now fighting for his life."

Cravens assured the beleaguered sheriff that the *News-Journal* would play the story about the beloved police K-9 front and center on the front page.

And then the publisher dropped the other shoe, telling his law enforcement buddy about the contingent of citizens who wanted to take out a full-page ad against him.

"And you're seriously thinking about publishing that piece of garbage, Jake? Do you know how hard my men are working on the Haynes murder case? It's priority one for this department. We know she was a church goin' mother, granny and great-granny. We know she was raped and brutalized. We know her family has been put through the ringer. And we know the community is scared and angry.

"But also know this, my friend. Me and my deputies will not rest till we find who raped and murdered her! That's my solemn promise to the taxpayers of Summer's Rest and Taylor County. A killer is on the loose out there. But we will catch him and bring him to justice. I give you my word on that." Coffmann spoke emphatically as he paced the polished concrete floor of his office. Then he gave the publisher a beseeching can-you-cut-me-an-ounce-of-slack look.

"I'll see what can do about that ad, Ethan, but no promises, understand?" Cravens took one last sip of his coffee and turned to leave.

"Understood," the sheriff said. "Now you be careful out there."

Then the sheriff said what he always said when the two of them parted. "Keep the swamp drained, Jake, so you can see the alligators. You never know when one of 'em's gonna' try to bite you in the ass."

"I'll do that," said the publisher, his eyes wandering to the four double-barreled shotguns in the gun rack on the wall behind the sheriff's desk.

Chapter 6
Painful Flashback

David Patrick Jackson III made his coffee—as he did every morning right away when he woke up. But first he tidied up his bed—pretty and tight as you please. He'd once had an ex-Marine friend who told him how every morning in basic training, Marine recruits had to make their beds so tight you could bounce a quarter off the sheets.

Though he knew darn well he'd never himself be a Marine, the daily ritual of making a tight bed somehow appealed to him. And so he did it faithfully every morning, soon as he rose. Then, before brewing his coffee, he fluffed his pillows. The pillow fluffing and bed making somehow helped him get centered—though at the same time he knew full well that only he would appreciate his neatness.

But that was okay. A shrink had told him that if neatness made him feel good about himself, then go for it!

"Be a neat freak, but be a damned good one, David!" the doctor had emphasized.

That therapist had had more degrees hanging on his wall than Carter's had stink pills. Even now, all these years later, David could still see the prison psychiatrist. Was his name Dr. Lu? Or could it have been Dr. Fu? David couldn't recall for certain but he did remember that the doctor looked to be as miserable and depressed as the inmates he counseled.

Bed made and coffee ready to sip, David sat staring out the window of his dingy, weather-beaten trailer. It was just a rental but it had served his purpose—at least up to now. The dilapidated trailer was totally secluded in a densely wooded area about a mile from the nearest road, an unpaved one at that. And it didn't even have a real door—only a thick quilt that he'd nailed to the frame of the opening, where a door should have been, to help keep out the chill. Come spring he reminded himself he'd make a real door to take its place—if he was here in the spring. He had nailed plastic over the structure's three dirty, broken windows.

His only heat: a tiny space heater he'd picked up for practically nothing at a garage sale a few weeks earlier. His water source: a gurgling stream a stone's throw away. His toilet: a crude, leaning outhouse that had likely been standing for 50 years.

His neighbors? He had none save for the occasional raccoon, possum, bobcat, deer, rabbit or squirrel. And of course there were those humming birds that had been attracted to the bird feeder just outside his sagging front porch. The tiny winged creatures fluttered about, made a whirring sound as they chirped and even, on occasion, locked eyes with him as he sipped his hot early morning brew. It was a good morning when they hovered for maybe up to 30 seconds and flashed him a glint of green.

He had no real neighbors—as in human beings—and that was just dandy with David Patrick Jackson III. Because people meant trouble. And man, were they ever nosy! They always asked questions. Wanted to know where he had come from. What he did for a living. Where he went to church. *Where I go to church of all things!*

And the nosiness and prying never stopped. He had learned the hard way that the more he shared with them, the more they could and would use against him. So here he lived. And not so much lived as meagerly existed. In a patch of remote, dark woods a long walk from the nearest road. A place that served his purpose well. An off-the-beaten-track place where a man could get lost and stay that way if he so chose. The perfect place to think and plan and try to put his sordid life back together.

He vowed to get something better once he got his feet on the ground. That meant finding a job, but not just any job. Not flipping burgers or painting barns or hammering nails or digging ditches or picking vegetables for some fatass rich farmer.

He would land a real job—not the tedious work he was doing with his hands now. Maybe something in a nice clean, air-conditioned office with thick carpet and soothing music or even a professional sales job where he'd wear a jacket and tie. Because he knew how to read people. How to make them let their guard down and do his bidding. *How to make them like me!*

And when he got that "real job," David Patrick Jackson III promised himself he'd "split the scene" from East Tennessee quicker than one of those humming birds could dart away.

But how to do all this when you were on probation—after pulling time in prison in North Carolina for murder? How to ever make people like him again and look up to him—as they did before he decapitated that no-good Mexican who'd tried to do him in?

Nobody hurts me! No wetback. Nobody. He got what he had comin' to him.

He even today got angry—and a tad scared—when he thought of how he'd been ambushed that late night all those years ago on a beach by two Hispanic men dressed in black. They had for sure wanted to kill him, but if they'd had their way, it wouldn't have been that simple. No, death would have been a relief considering what torture they had had in mind for him.

Now, as he thought about it, he didn't even want to imagine how horrible it all could have turned out.

It could have been ugly. Really ugly. *But surprise!*

This old rascal had turned the tables on them.

Had gotten the draw on them and sent one of the Mexicans to an early grave. But damned if the other scoundrel hadn't gotten away!

And when there's a witness who can rat on you, and fill a courtroom with a pack of lies, you've got trouble. Big trouble.

As in winding up in a stinkin', filthy state prison in West Tabor City, North Carolina—about a 45-minute drive from the beaches and crashing waves of the Atlantic Ocean.

But like the hundreds of others incarcerated in that prison, he never laid eyes on the majestic beaches or blue ocean waves that were so tantalizingly close. When the wind was just right, you might get a hint of taste of the salt air, and some of the inmates even claimed they could hear the ocean when all was completely still.

But for Jackson, in the 12 years he spent in virtual solitude at that remote North Carolina prison, he never heard or smelled or touched any part of the sea. All he had was his imagination of how he thought the mighty, magnificent Atlantic looked and sounded.

The man who had taken a life to defend himself against certain death by those two Mexicans hadn't laid eyes on those beaches even after he'd gotten out of prison. Because he'd convinced himself that revisiting the ocean would bring back too many memories. Some of them sweet, but some very bad.

And no point in dredging up the painful past.

Then again, the man who had savagely had his way with Hazel Eula Haynes, to no avail, since the old woman had pathetically little money and absolutely no pain pills, narrowly escaped being assaulted.

His close call had come behind the drab gray walls of the state prison in West Tabor City.

It had happened during the first year of his time behind bars. Two Mexican inmates had decided they wanted to have their way—"to have a little fun with him" as one of them would later confess. David Patrick Jackson III had seemed like easy prey. And besides, the news grapevine around the joint was that he had cut a Mexican to pieces. Time, they figured, for him to get his payback.

It hadn't taken much for the two convicted murderers—lifers and perennial troublemakers at the prison—to convince the guards to look the other way one summer night. *So damned easy to win over a boring, tired, under-paid guard with a few prime buds of marijuana.*

And so the disgruntled guards in charge of Jackson's cellblock were nowhere to be seen or heard when the two, who had nothing to lose, made their play.

Not that any of the other inmates in that cellblock would have said a word or cried for help—even if they'd seen or heard what was coming down. That's because the sacred code of a prison population is that a snitch of any kind won't live long.

As it happened, Jackson had not been victimized. Had, unbeknownst to his two attackers, razor-sharp chisels. He had found them in the cabinet shop where he worked and had tucked them in a tiny slit in his mattress. So when they made their move, surprise! He cut them quickly and deeply and blood ran like a river. Then came their agonizing screams for mercy. But their would-be prey wouldn't stop the bloodletting. He kept slashing them again and again. And he did it while he laughed and spit on them and cursed them. Like a wild, crazed maniac bent on extracting his pound of flesh.

No one, after that full-moon night, ever bothered David Patrick Jackson III again. They didn't visit with him nor did they eat with him or worship with him or associate with him in any way. In the exercise yard, everyone—even the guards—kept their distance from the man who had turned the tables on those who had tried to hurt him.

And so David Patrick Jackson III had effectively pulled his time behind bars in solitude. He had never had a visitor—from the inside or from the outside. He trusted no one, and no one trusted him, let alone dared hurt him.

There had been what amounted to a pseudo inquiry by prison authorities into the chisel cutting incident, but in the end the near-retirement warden—inwardly glad that the two troublesome lifers had been hurt so—had turned a blind eye. Good riddance to those cretins. And what a relief that they got what they deserved—seemed to be the warden's attitude. They had been shipped off to some sort of hospital and never heard from again by those at the prison in West Tabor City.

And what punishment was levied on David Patrick Jackson III? Not so much as a slap on the wrist, although they did grill him about how he'd come by those chisels. He had told investigators the God's honest truth about finding the sharpened tools in the cabinet shop and said they'd been sent there to him from the Almighty. And they'd bought it—glad again to be rid of the pair of troublemakers.

After that, word spread quickly through the prison that a very dangerous "chisel man" had had his way with two of the worst inmates who had ever been locked up there. No one would ever again mess with "chisel man." They left him alone. Kept their distance and some of them even went out of their way to do him favors. He liked being by himself and not connected to anyone. Just fine with him to do his time not worrying about anyone or anything else.

But, reflecting on it now: *So many years lost! Such a nasty, rotten prison in nowhere, North Carolina, to waste away all that time.*

Finally, he had been paroled and put on probation and allowed, with permission from his probation officer, to leave the state of North Carolina. Because North Carolina had, in truth, grown weary of warehousing such a dangerous inmate, and glory be, a distant cousin in East Tennessee hadn't given up on him and believed that everyone deserved a second chance—regardless of what misdeed they had done. The soft-hearted, gullible cousin had arranged for his wayward kin to occupy this primitive, minimal abode in the wilderness, and he'd even found him work as a carpenter.

And what had the opportunistic, desperate ex-con done?

He had eagerly taken his cousin up on his offer and moved to the mountains of East Tennessee—where he had never even visited in his 35 years of living—and he had promised the authorities, but not himself, to never, ever again bother a soul.

And what of his savior cousin? Poor fellow seemed to be proof that good deeds don't necessarily come back to you. Because not longer than one week after David Patrick Jackson III had arrived in East Tennessee—the cousin had collapsed and died from a cardiac arrest. Thus, the one living soul connected with the ex-con in this mountain community was gone.

So Jackson, now truly all alone, had made the best of it. Not that he had tried to blend in, so to speak, with his new community. Far from it. He had kept to himself—his only contact with people being for whatever he could get out of them, be that payment for labor he performed or hot food from a local church pantry. At the latter, the apron-clad, cheery-faced women running it never asked questions. Didn't seem to care one bit about who he was or what he had or didn't have. Which was just fine and dandy with him, because the best people, for David Patrick Jackson III, were those who minded their own business and paid him no attention.

His pledge to the parole board and to his overworked, tired probation officer: *Forget the dead Mexican. Forget that self-defense chisel stuff in the joint. I'm a reformed man. I've been rehabilitated. I'm healed. And I'm ready to be a productive, law-abiding, upright citizen.*

People would believe anything. They were so gullible, so dumb, so easily persuaded. He'd even read that one of Adolph Hitler's top henchmen in Nazi Germany had once declared that the bigger the lie, the more people believed it.

He took a last sip of his coffee and intently watched another humming bird dart so quickly in two different directions. Then he reflected once again on how it had all come down that night he had stealthily broke into the home of the vulnerable, sleeping Hazel Eula Haynes. He had always been a masterful lock picker—from his early crime spree days in North Carolina—and the only door to his victim's trailer had been a piece of cake.

He had entered quietly about two in the morning, sure that he'd find a stockpile of prescription opioids—the drugs of choice for hurting folks in rural Appalachia. Because hadn't he overheard her, from his adjacent booth at McDonald's in Summer's Rest, complaining about her back and her gums? About swallowing pills of hydrocodone every day to cope with the pain?

A feller can learn a right smart bit just by keepin' his ears cocked and his mouth shut.

But instead of opioids, he found an old, wrinkled woman sleeping like a baby among hundreds of books, magazines and church bulletins. And what about all those framed pictures of what must have been her kids and grand-kids and in-laws? They practically covered the paneled walls of her trailer.

And the cards—birthday cards, anniversary cards, Christmas cards, Valentine's Day cards, cards for Easter and Thanksgiving. Hazel Eula Haynes apparently cherished them and saved every last one of them.

There, too, were letters of warm thanks from Christian organizations like Samaritan's Purse or from nationally known, well-heeled ministers like Will Graham, Joel Osteen and Rick Warren. The woman apparently had a soft spot in her heart for so-called messengers of God. *Either that,* her killer had thought cynically that early morning of his crime, *or she'd been trying to buy her way into Heaven.*

A typical old horder, he thought, recollecting what he encountered during his break-in. *Never, ever got rid of a letter, picture or card. A granny who lived for her family, her church and her friends.*

And what'd it all amount to? The only pill bottle on her bedside table indeed had a label for a hydrocodone prescription, but it was empty.

And so he had hurt her badly—not because he had planned to do that, but it just somehow happened. He had come for pills and money, and he had struck out on both counts.

He had become angry and frustrated. So much so, that he gagged the startled woman when he woke her up—her eyes bulging with terror and her frail body shaking. He shook her. He slapped her. He strangled her, and then he did the worst thing you can imagine to a 90-year-old woman. He did not enjoy it at all, but it just seemed, to him—in all his rage—that it was the thing to do at the time.

And no, he didn't mean to kill her. That, in his mind, was just an unintended, unfortunate consequence. He didn't like himself for doing that, but so be it. It was a done deed, and, besides, he had gotten away with it. Clean as you please. As in being free as a bird.

He figured the bird would stay free because he had left absolutely not one iota of evidence. No fingerprints cause he'd worn gloves. And no DNA because he'd made off with her nightgown, bedsheets, pillow cases, blanket and quilt. *And not one drop of my semen on or in 'er cause I slipped outta her just in time.*

Nothing to tie him to the crime scene.

Yep, this old sly knife and chisel man outsmarted 'em and got away with murder, but damn, I wish she'd had some of them pills. And it had all been so easy, he thought. *As easy as feeding my humming birds. I didn't feel a thing? Guilt? None. Fear? Not a twinge. Loss of sleep from what I did? This old fella's been sleepin' like a baby! Restlessness? Ain't never been calmer in my life.*

Chapter 7
Searching for a Killer

Back at his office, Taylor County High Sheriff Ethan Coffmann worked feverishly to find the still-at-large murderer. His challenge: No promising leads, aside from scant evidence left at the crime scene—the inside of Hazel Eula Haynes' trailer.

Whoever had so brutally assaulted her had covered his tracks pretty well—as if they'd never been there. There were no fingerprints, other than Miz Hazel's or members of her family, left in her trailer. No palm or finger smudges on the windows or doors. No signs of forced entry. The door lock had not been jammed or forced. It was as if the intruder had a key and easily gained access.

In addition, there had been no witnesses. Not one of the victim's neighbors could recall hearing or seeing anything out of the ordinary during the time frame of the assault and murder. Which was to be expected. Most of them, like their ill-fated neighbor, were up in years, and had turned in by nine or 10 that night. They were typical East Tennessee senior citizens—in bed early, watching Fox News and rising with the chickens the next morning.

On top of all this, the murderer apparently had the moxie not to leave any of his DNA at the crime scene. The victim's bedsheets, blankets, nightgown and even the pillow cases on her pillows had been removed by the perpetrator.

But who could have committed this crime? That's what stumped Sheriff Coffmann. He tried to clear his mind and keep things simple—returning to the three basic elements underpinning most any crime: Motive, opportunity and means.

The first element—motive—puzzled him. Why would someone

have assaulted and killed her? She had very little money. No jewelry or valuables worth stealing. No deep, dark secrets that she harbored that Sheriff Coffmann knew of. No drugs, other than her pain medicines, and no known enemies. In fact, far as he could tell, she was just a sweet old church-going lady much beloved by her family and others—even strangers who had needed a helping hand.

It was true that Hazel Eula Haynes had prescriptions for painkillers, and certain unseemly kinds of individuals in East Tennessee would do just about anything to feed their appetite for opioids. Sheriff Coffmann knew for a fact that drug overdoses and suicide and crime rates in Appalachia were much higher in these mountains than in other parts of the U.S. Studies had linked those grim rates to misuse of opioid painkillers.

Still, he couldn't fathom that someone would kill an innocent old woman for thinking she might have a bottle of hydrocodone. Which, it turned out, she didn't have, according to a search of her premises and according to her pharmacist who told deputies that her prescription had expired and been renewed just the day before. He had expected her to come in for a refill the day after she was killed.

And did the murderer have opportunity? Yes, plenty of it, the sheriff figured.

The totally vulnerable victim lived alone, in an old trailer. The front door, her daughters assured the sheriff, had been locked before she turned in. Their creature-of-habit mother always locked her door before she went to bed. Nevertheless, it wouldn't have taken Houdini to breach that thin, metal door with what appeared to be a flimsy, outdated lock mechanism.

As for the murdered woman's neighbors? Interviewed the next day, they all said they had been asleep during the time frame of the murder and the crime shocked and frightened them as much as it did everyone else.

And the perpetrator had the means to commit his deed. He had killed the old woman, who apparently had put up a struggle, with his bare hands. A frail 110 pounds, she hadn't stood a chance against surely a bigger, stronger, more muscular foe. The sheriff figured her assailant had gone into a maniacal rage when he couldn't find any pain pills or money, and so he decided to take away what last shred of decency she had. He raped her, brutally and repeatedly. Did he laugh or brag why he did this? Crushed her little hands in his or grabbed her by the hair of her head? Had she been, to him, some kind of fleshly consolation prize?

But then again, what man would sexually assault a 90-year-old feeble, skin and bone woman? And a woman, at that, who probably fought him with every fiber in her small body. The sheriff could imagine the terrified Miz Hazel clawing and kicking and punching and screaming, and even begging for mercy—all to no avail. Because the nighttime heinous visitor who had targeted her was big, strong, relentless and had absolutely no conscience. He had latched onto his helpless prey and it had been no use for her. Even if she had screamed—and the sheriff was sure in his mind that she had—no one heard.

Hitting a dry well for solid leads, Sheriff Coffmann had enlisted the aid of the Behavioral Analysis Unit of the FBI. He had asked the unit to create a social and psychological profile of the murderer.

Some of his top deputies had scoffed at this idea, dismissing the profile work of the BAU as little more than "smoke and mirrors." And the sheriff himself realized the controversy associated with creating a profile of suspects who commit certain kinds of crimes. Naysayers of profiling asserted that criminals were as varied and unpredictable as grains of sands on a beach; you were only fooling yourself if you thought you could construct a truly revealing profile of a wanted person.

Still, the sheriff thought it worth a try. Because the only thing he knew for certain—or thought he knew for sure—was that the person he was looking for was a man.

But maybe, now that he thought more about it, the supposed man might even have been what they called in East Tennessee a "he/she." Part man and part woman? Transgender?

Anything was possible, and that only further confounded the under-fire high sheriff of Taylor County.

Coffmann considered his next move. He already had every sworn law enforcement officer in Taylor County looking for leads. A half dozen of his deputies had interviewed and reinterviewed every one of her family members. Forensics investigators from outside his department had not only combed the interior of the victim's trailer; with the help of crime-sniffing dogs, they'd been over every foot of the terrain in her yard and within 300 yards of her property. Lastly, his officers had gotten their fair share of false tips—every one of which they'd had to follow up on—just in case.

There was the tip from a distant cousin of the deceased. Miz Hazel's daughters hadn't heard nor seen him in at least 20 years, but the man swore that there'd been bad blood between Miz Hazel and one of her sons-in-law—stemming from how the in-law had once, in an angry fit, packed his things, including his clothes, hunting dog and hightailed it to the beach, leaving his pregnant wife to fend for herself.

Yes, the malcontent had packed up and left but he'd returned, sunburned, hungry, lonely and head held low, within a few weeks. And the couple had made up and even renewed their marriage vows—at, of all places, the beach. And Hazel Eula Haynes? Amazingly, she had wrapped her spindly arms around him and welcomed him back into the family.

There had been the tip that a wayward grandson had stolen Miz Hazel's checkbook, and, forging her signature, had written checks which were cashed at the Walmart in Summer's Rest and at a local convenience store.

To the chagrin of authorities, the woman had refused to press charges against her shamed, tattooed grandson; had instead forgiven him and taken him to church with her. She had done so even after her name had been listed on a humiliating "Do Not Cash Their Check" list posted at a local convenience store. Law enforcement considered all this and decided to eliminate the grandson as a suspect.

And police even had received an anonymous tip that while in her twenties, Miz Hazel had been an exotic dancer in a nightclub in Richmond, Virginia. The tipster said the entire family knew about this well-kept secret and knew, as well, about the sinister types of lusting men who stuffed ten-dollar bills in her bikini bottom.

When police followed up, they found that, yes, there was some truth to the fact that the murder victim had gone through a semi-wild stage in her youth, but no, there was no evidence she'd ever been a stripper or dancer of any kind. To the contrary, after having to get married at the age of 16—and then losing the baby—she had turned her life completely around. She had left the "no count scumbag who got her pregnant and then she got saved," as one of her longtime confidantes put it to police.

"She became a different person—devoting her life to Jesus and to her church," the confidante said.

Maybe the most tantalizing tip involved a 72-year-old man minding his own business and working at the local animal shelter. He had become a person of interest to police after it was disclosed that he had escaped from prison 30 years earlier. He had stayed on the straight and narrow all those years on the lamb—working for nothing, except his room and board, as a volunteer at homeless shelters and pitching in at numerous Habitat for Humanity projects. He had been sentenced and served time in prison for armed robbery of a convenience store, had escaped and had finally been caught, just by accident, when a retired deputy sheriff seemed to vaguely recognize him. The lawman had run his picture through facial recognition software, and there he was—an escaped but gentle and friendly convict living in Summer's Rest and wanted by the state of North Carolina.

However, Coffmann had been deeply skeptical that the escapee was their murderer. For one thing, the ex-con didn't even begin to fit the FBI's profile of who they were looking for: white, athletic and strong, at least six feet tall, a passive-aggressive, deranged loner who avoided contact with wider society, a man without a shred of a conscience, a person who likely had physically hurt a member of his own family or who himself had been hurt by one of his parents.

The ex-con person of interest had been anything but detached and disturbed. He'd been a back-patting, handshaking regular at the weekly Saturday car show in downtown Summer's Rest. At the Girl Scout cookies stand, he'd cheerfully bought every box left on the table at day's end and left a generous tip.

Tip after tip hadn't led Coffmann's men to anything substantial. And as the hunt continued to bear no fruit, a small but vocal minority of citizens of Taylor County grew more fearful, restless and demanding.

Day by day, they became more obnoxious, demanding that whoever killed granny Haynes be arrested, charged, locked up, tried and convicted and executed. No matter that a suspect, even if indicted, is innocent until proven guilty by a jury of his peers.

"Pert near ninety percent of them that's brung in by the POH-LICE is guity as sin," one old gentleman opined at Susie's Diner. "And why they ain't got nary a suspect in this here murder case is just plumb unbelieveable."

High Sheriff Coffmann knew better than anyone else that the public pressure for his office to make an arrest was reaching a fever pitch. He was certain it would only get worse. And what of his good friend Jake Cravens, publisher of the local community newspaper? Though he and Cravens were buddies, the publisher would have no choice but to soon cave to that up-and-arms group that wanted to buy a full page ad in the newspaper.

Coffmann could imagine what the ad would scream—in large, bold headlines: That the sheriff's office, once the pride and joy of Taylor County, had become a sham. That Coffmann and his deputies could never catch "the big fish" drug dealers—always instead arresting the young folks caught smoking marijuana or making meth in the back of their cars. That Coffmann's jail had become a joke—a revolving door for lawbreakers in Taylor County who got arrested, were jailed, made bond and then were set loose—free as birds—to break the law again and again. That there had been rumors (not true but how does one go about dispelling them completely?) that Coffmann himself was having problems at home with his own family so how could he be expected to manage his deputies and jailers? That it was way past time for a "drain-the-swamp" change in law enforcement in Taylor County. That Coffmann had at first been given the benefit of the doubt but now he and his men had become the laughingstock of the town—unable, as one self-declared hard working concerned taxpayer put it—"to even catch a cold." And lastly, that the murderer who so brutally took the life of Hazel Eula Haynes was running around free as you please and ready to strike again.

Chapter 8
Clearing the Air

Never one to like the tedious, mind-numbing paperwork of arrests, warrants and jailings, or the administrative details of running his office, the high sheriff of Taylor County escaped to his police cruiser. It was a gorgeous late fall day—the mountains framing Summer's Rest a canvas of brilliant golds, reds, browns and greens. Nature's paint brush had also transformed the town's trees into a plethora of stunning colors. All the leaves would be gone soon. Even now, they had begun fluttering in the light breeze to the ground.

Because he hadn't visited, for quite a while, a part of the community called "Black Cat Town," he decided to take a spin over that way. "Black Cat Town," as it was known throughout Summer's Rest, was a hangover name from before the Civil Rights Movement of the 1960s. It had been the home, more than half a century ago, for the all-black (called all-Negro at the time), DeWayne School, where African Americans in Summer's Rest and in adjoining towns rode buses to attend.

In the mid to late 1960s, things had begun to change—glacially in some instances but change, nonetheless. Because all those black children who had been bused—some as far as 50 miles from Summer's Rest—to the DeWayne School in Black Cat Town—were allowed to go to white schools.

"They just liked going to their own school in Black Cat Town," an elderly local woman had reminisced with Coffman recently. "It weren't about racism or nothin' like that. That's just the way things was back then."

Coffmann turned his police cruiser down a side street of Black

Cat Town. He drove slowly, noticing that most of the yards of the little row houses seemed to be kept clear of trash. And the dwellings themselves, while modest, seemed to be livable and well kept. Porches were swept clean and dogs were kept behind fences or in cages. The area definitely didn't smack of the decay and bleakness—and rampant crime—of some of America's big inner city neighborhoods. Still, it was Black Cat Town—a far stretch from the upscale, well-manicured, lushly green golf course community just a short drive away.

"How you boys doin' today?" he called out to two light-skinned kids—maybe 12 or 13 years old—shooting hoops at the lone basketball goal in the back lot of the Fire Faith Holiness Church. It had been the first "colored church" founded in Northeast Tennessee—by a Godly ex-slave preacher whose vision had been to establish a place where Negroes could worship and find divine refuge from racial injustice, lynching and all manner of other attacks.

"We be just fine, suh," said the littlest one of them. "We's hopin' to grow up to be just like King James!"

"Well, you just might do that!" the grinning sheriff shouted back to them.

His eyes wandered to the historic little church, a safe-haven sanctuary where generations of blacks had connected with God and exercised their charismatic form of worship—back clapping, dancing, hugging, kissing, shouting "Praise the Lord!"

Then he sat back and watched the two boys, each with their ball cap on backwards and their sweaty t-shirts hanging almost to their knees, attacking the goal. The net had long since been torn down, and the pavement they bounced their ball on was cracked with weeds sprouting up every few feet. But they were having fun, talking "smack" to one another and occasionally stopping to give each other a high five.

The sheriff gave the two scruffy boys a thumbs up and parting wave and between bouncing their ball they waved back.

He made a quick radio check with headquarters.

"Everything is A-Ok here, Sheriff," Mattie assured him. "You just enjoy that nice weather out there today."

"Ten-four," he replied. But inside he had an unsettled feeling. He always felt that way, it seemed, when he got word that everything was running along smoothly—without him. That old saying about when the cat is away the mouse will play…

He headed back toward the heart of Summer's Rest, passing, within a few minutes, War Memorial Park in the middle of town. If anyone doubted that the town he served was a patriotic community that cherished its veterans, all they had to do was visit this park. It was a reverential place where thousands of names of locals who had served in the military were etched in granite. The names included more than two dozen who had died in Vietnam. Also inscribed in stone there, among Old Glory and the state flag of Tennessee: the names of vets who paid the ultimate price in World War I, World War II, Korea, the Gulf and Afghanistan.

The high sheriff wondered whether someday his name, too, would find its way onto the shining granite wall. *And what of Delmar Greer,* he wondered. Doubtful that anyone from his blood kin—if he even had any such kin that still claimed him—would fork out the $50 fee to see that he was memorialized. *A damned shame*, Coffmann thought.

Coffmann parked his car near the town's historic wooden covered bridge. Built in the late 19th century from timber cut in the mountains and hauled here by rail and wagon, the bridge was now closed to traffic. However, the structure was a frequently-visited, historic landmark of East Tennessee. It had been photographed or painted many times, had been the subject of stories and legends and had even spawned a thriving summer "Covered Bridge Festival" teeming with music, vendors, food and arts and crafts.

Ignoring the crackling of his radio, Coffmann got out of his police cruiser and walked to a bench near the bridge. The air was cool and crisp—typical for an early day in November—and the sky was overcast with a few gray clouds. Earlier that day, the sun had gotten brighter. Right now, however, it was nowhere to be seen.

But Coffmann didn't mind the gloominess. He just wanted to be alone. To reflect and contemplate his next move in the daunting murder case that threatened to end his up-to-this point illustrious career in law enforcement. What would he do financially if he were drummed out of office? As High Sheriff of Taylor County, his yearly salary was $85,000—not a king's ransom but enough so that his wife Laura could stay home, cook their meals and tend to their two young sons. And that figure, he kept reminding himself, was a lot higher than what he started at in law enforcement—as a traffic cop writing tickets and filling out accident reports. *So long ago being just a cop trying to catch speeders and writing up shoplifters at Walmart,* he reminded himself. *But in some ways just like yesterday.*

Right now, surprisingly but perfectly suiting the sheriff, the area around the covered bridge was deserted. No children frolicked about in the nearby play area. No young couples held hands while they stared dreamily at the gentle, shallow, cold river flowing beneath the bridge. No ducks floated contentedly down the river. No one leaned over the footbridge trying to spot a fish. Because it was too cold, no picnickers lazed about on their blankets with their folding chairs, baskets of food, coolers and Frisbees.

At the end of a row of weeping willows, and providing shade for the play area, a massive oak tree caught Coffmann's attention. Its branches, which had almost lost all their leaves, seemed to claw at the air like macabre tentacles. The sheriff decided not to sit down but to keep walking, his boots disturbing the rustling, crunchy leaves that by now had covered the ground. Soon the leaves would be gone—replaced practically before he knew it—with snow and ice. And then, if he walked here again, he'd be shuffling through the white stuff. Bundled up rambunctious children would no doubt be loving it—building snowmen and throwing snowballs and sliding around and doing whatever kids do to enjoy winter. Sooner or later it would warm up, however, and the snowy landscape near the river would get sloppy. No matter. The kids would still love to play in the quickly melting whiteness.

Coffmann found another wooden bench and sat. The quiet and stillness seemed almost spiritual—just what he needed to exhale and get his bearings. He cast his eyes upward toward one of the ridges east of town. On top of it were three white crosses with the words, immediately beneath the crosses, in big red letters: "JESUS IS LORD."

Coffmann had seen those crosses and those words countless times, and he'd never paid them much heed. Now, however, they seemed to be trying to speak to his heart. To what had always been a hardened, skeptical heart, a heart that had not had much time for church or God or the Bible.

All those sorts of things, Coffmann had tolerated and even, on occasion, had respected and tangentially participated in (especially in his campaigns when it had been incumbent upon him to make polite appearances at church suppers). The more he thought about it, he hadn't been a very good believer. At best, the high sheriff of Taylor County had been a lukewarm Christian, going to church many a Sunday but never really understanding why. He had gone through the churchly motions, but if anyone in Taylor County, Tennessee, was a cool, collected, detached, don't-bother-me Christian, it was Ethan Coffmann.

The more he dwelled on it, the more mysterious and ungraspable all this business of faith, the Bible and eternal life, or, as the case might be, eternal damnation, struck him.

Coffmann reflected on the time, when he was only 13, that he had been practically dragged by his parents to answer the call to baptism and be "saved." He had been led by the one-handed (and scary to him, as a boy) Preacher Samuel Prichard and fully immersed—all those years ago—in the river he now stared at.

"You ain't been saved, till you go all the way under the water!" his finger-pointing stern grandmother had warned him. "And none of this sprinklin' stuff that them Cath-O-Licks do. They ain't a bit more saved than the devil hisself."

Though he had been raised by upstanding, devoted-to-their-church Christian parents, some things still baffled him. Why did some folks raise their hands—like they were waving at something or somebody above—when hymns were sung in church services? Why did the preacher drive a brand new car, make his rounds in a suit and tie and live in a nice parsonage? All this while some sunken-faced members of his flock made due in ratty trailers and wore hand-me-downs?

And speaking of the preacher, why was it that when his parents had the fat man over for a meal right after Sunday church, he got first dibs on the fried chicken? Why'd he always have the big plump breast, when Ethan and his two younger brothers had to settle for wings, backs or necks?

And why was there so much evil and darkness in this world? Coffmann had seen the worst of it: murder, wife-beatings, kidnappings, suicides, thievery—all manner of brokenness and malignancy of humanity in the community where he tried to keep people safe and put the bad folks behind bars. It was always an uphill struggle. Even when you brought some law-breaker to justice, justice wasn't necessarily meted out. The overworked, tired judges were often too lenient—opting to give those who broke the law only a slap on the wrist. That was because Coffmann's jail was almost always full of the worst of the worst—killers, rapists, child molesters. So a judge, even if he wanted to, frequently had no place to incarcerate someone who stole a car, broke into a home or absconded with someone's painkillers.

Just a few miles up the road, in a neighboring county, a young couple had been shot dead while sleeping in their bed. The bizarre case, attracting national attention, had been dubbed the Facebook catfish murders because the ruthless killings had stemmed from an online feud and false identity.

Thank God those didn't happen on my watch, Coffmann thought. *As if I didn't have enough to worry about without cyber crimes.*

Somehow, in the midst of all these troubling ruminations, Coffmann couldn't take his eyes off those three white crosses. There was something different about them on this otherwise bleak, foreboding gray day. Something uplifting. Coffmann couldn't put his finger on it exactly, but he thought he felt some sort of admonition from God.

But what was it?

Can you sense something profound and instructive from God but not understand it? the sheriff wondered. He looked around to make sure no one was nearby.

No one was. All was quiet, except for the sound of the mountain river—a hint of whitewater at the small waterfall near the bridge. Soon enough, wintry ice melt would be making that water too cold to wade in.

The words of his late beloved mother came back to him: *Be true to your core, son. Know who you are. Be yourself. You are you. Unique, No one else in the universe, past or present, is just like you. You can do anything you set your mind to. Never forget that.*

Why had he thought of that inspiration—just now after all these years?

Emboldened, High Sheriff Ethan Coffmann had no answer to that question, but now he did know one thing. He could do this. He could solve this case. He would prevail. He would bring Hazel Eula Haynes' murderer to justice if it was the last thing he ever did. *And it just might well be,* he thought.

Chapter 9

The Local Press Investigates

We're doing the best we can, ma'am. You know, we don't make the news, we just report it," *News-Journal* editor Dudley Lowery politely said.

But the impetuous woman with teased hair and too much makeup in the editor's office wouldn't be deterred. "Well, y'all could keep this crime and what our no-good-for-nothin', triflin' sheriff is doin' to solve it on the front page—ever blessed day!

"And if you ain't gonna do that, I'll cancel my *prescription* taday! And I ain't the only one'll cancel."

"Ma'am, like I said, we print what we can find out from the authorities and our other sources. But I give you my word of honor: we won't let this story die."

Haggard from being up late that previous night, as he was most nights of his 60-hour grueling work week, Lowery tried his best to calm her. But the more he explained the newspaper's position, the less his listener seemed to like it. And for whatever reason, an old saying from Mark Twain popped up in his mind: *I am not the editor of a newspaper and shall always try to do right and be good so that God will not make me one.* Right at the moment, the *News-Journal*'s editor wished he'd chosen another profession.

With angular features, deep blue eyes, hippyish light brown hair and a thin face with just a hint of a mustache, Lowery could have passed for a modern-day Ichabod Crane. He had been hired three years ago at the *News-Journal* and had ascended quickly to his position as Jake Cravens' number one person in the newsroom. Helping him in that climb were his excellent journalism skills and the paper's high turnover of lowly paid reporters. He also possessed that rare trait for a journalist today—personal warmth. To put it mildly, most people instantly liked Lowery, and that was exactly what the publisher wanted in an editor. He was an astute listener, easily connected with folks, even those who disagreed with his positions on the editorial page, and had been won over by the charm and friendliness of living in a small town.

But the venomous complainant he confronted now would not be placated. The sharp-nosed, snarling woman, rolls of fat jiggling from her belly and her arms flapping in exasperation, demanded to see the editor's "bossman."

"That would be me, ma'am," said Cravens, who had overheard her outburst of anger.

She had caused a stir in the low-ceilinged newsroom, where even faint sounds got magnified. The *News-Journal*'s three full time reporters had paused in their cubicled work areas from tapping on their Mac computers and scribbling in their notebooks. Their attention piqued when they noticed the publisher, not at all happy that his newsroom had been disrupted, stepped out of his office.

"Now you see here—you can rest assured we are staying on top of the sheriff's investigation of this murder case. And, as to my editor here, he's like a bloodhound. If there's anything a'tall that he thinks is bein' covered up about this case, or not bein' done right by Sheriff Coffmann, he'll blow the lid right off of it."

The woman dug in: "Well, what exactly is it that y'all plan to do with your newspaper to help solve this crime? I hear tell all over town that you 'n the sheriff's drinkin' buddies and that you helped get him elected with your newspaper in the first place."

Taken aback for a few seconds, the publisher gathered himself and spoke. "Ma'am, I take very seriously the role of the press—that bein', when you get right down to it, mostly my newspaper —to report the news fairly, truthfully and with the highest integrity. That means nobody, and I do mean nobody, tells me what to do with the *News-Journal.*

"And as to my esteemed editor here, Mr. Lowery, I hired him because of his high credentials in journalism and because he believes same as me. The First Amendment to the Constitution of the United States cannot be bought, ma'am."

"I ain't carin' nothin' about the right to bear arms!" the woman, her anger peaking, shot back. "Me an' mine's already got our guns and nobody better dare fool with us!"

"Ma'am, that's the Second Amendment to the Constitution you're talkin' about," said Cravens, biting his lips to keep a straight face. Then he decided not to pursue educating her about freedom of the press *because it'd just be a waste of breath,* he figured.

Grimacing, she whipped the strap of her pocketbook back over her shoulder, mumbled her discontent and did an about-face out the door.

When they were sure she had left the newsroom, Cravens asked his editor to accompany him. Closing the door to his office, the publisher said he wanted to have a "friendly chat" with Lowery on how best to cover the talk-of-the-town murder case.

"You know, young man, that I've always believed in pursuing the truth with my newspaper, and I know sometimes that can be a right slippery thing to try to do. Because, what is that old saying about coming up with the truth? 'Gettin' the truth all depends on whose ox is bein' gored.'"

"I'm not sure what you mean by that, sir," Lowery replied. "I was taught that a journalist ALWAYS is after the truth. Regardless of whose reputation might take a hit…"

"That's well and good—up to a point," Cravens said. "But you have to remember, this is a small town. We, meanin' you and me and our families, have got no place to hide. We see our readers in the grocery store. We go to church with them. Our children attend school with their children. We attend their families' weddings and graduations and funerals and they do the same with us.

"What I'm saying, son, is that practicin' journalism in a small town is different. There's certain sensitivities that have to be taken into account… As an old friend publisher of mine way out in South Dakota put it: "With a small town newspaper, you've got to be hard nosed and soft hearted."

Lowery, who had been assured when he was hired that no story was off limits for the *News-Journal*, began to feel uncomfortable. "You yourself, sir, told that woman that the First Amendment is not for sale."

His face reddening, Cravens snapped back. "Now don't you start lecturin' me about what I can or can't do with my newspaper! I had ink in my blood before you were in your mother's womb. And my granddaddy schooled me in the press when I was a printer's devil. Hell fire! You probably don't even know what a printer's devil was. Way before your time, boy."

The editor maintained eye contact but said nothing.

"And if there's one damned thing I believe about journalism, it's this: You don't burn a town down. You build it up." Cravens took a silk handkerchief from inside his suit jacket pocket and dabbed at the perspiration on his forehead. "Now you've got me all riled up and I wasn't meanin' to do that, but hear me out, please."

"Yes sir," said Lowery, squirming slightly in his chair.

"You're paid to do my biddin' and that means you're to find and report the news of this community and you're to do it objectively and fairly and to the best of your ability. And you're never to be bullied or dissuaded by anyone who wants you to cover up a story. Because I take pride in the fact that this newspaper is a respected, valued, strong institution."

Lowery said nothing but he couldn't help but think of the *News-Journal*'s steadily declining circulation and advertising revenue—troubling trends spawned largely from advertisers and readers being drawn *away* from the local newspaper and *toward* social media.

"Be that as it may, let me tell you a little story, young man. You listenin'?"

Cravens' editor nodded respectfully.

"When I was gettin' started in journalism—as a cub reporter and before my daddy took over the paper—my first big investigative story was about a local man who owned a full service repair shop and gas station.

"Somebody called me—who asked not to be named— and tipped me off about what they said was a bit of hanky panky involvin' the owner of that gas station and the city council.

"Well, to make a long story short, it seemed that the gas station owner was good friends with a couple of long-time serving city council members—so good that they made sure that owner was the sole business servicing all the police department's and sheriff's department's vehicles. A contract worth hundreds of thousands of dollars a year. Without even having to submit a bid.

"Are you with me, son? Are you followin' what I'm sayin'?"

"I'm listening, sir. Had that happened today, I'd say that'd be a big story. The *News-Journal* would be all over it."

Cravens answered: "That's what I thought. I was young, idealistic, full of piss and vinegar, fresh out of journalism school, my heart set on one day being a foreign correspondent and hot on the trail of any big story I could find. I wanted to win writing prizes and make my mark in the profession. I wanted—as to who said it in the movies?—TO BE SOMEBODY."

Lowery interjected, "Marlon Brandon said that, sir, in the movie On the Waterfront."

"You were always a smart one, weren't you, young man?" Cravens, lighting a cigar, quipped. "Here's the rest of my story. Well, it seems, the more I dug into this hanky panky business between that gas station owner and his cronies on the city council, the more dirt I found. The council hadn't put that lucrative contract up for bid in many years.

"So I wrote about that, and you know what happened, Mr. Lowery?"

The intrigued editor said he didn't but would guess that his boss's watchdog-like story sent shock waves through the community.

Cravens told him he was right—about the local shock waves. But as to the community rallying around the newspaper and celebrating the fact that the light of truth was shined on a shadowy illicit deal between the city council and that station owner? That didn't happen. In fact, much to the contrary.

The bristling city council called a special open meeting, inviting citizens to come and comment on the questioned contract.

People came in force and they spoke up forcefully—in support of their longtime friend and neighbor Howard Prickett, who owned the gas station. It seemed Mr. Prickett had funded scholarships at the high school, made large donations to the local Boy Scouts and Girl Scouts, and had generously supported several churches' food pantries. There was also story after story about how he'd helped so many down and out folks behind the scenes. He had been the model of a giving, selfless, Christian citizen in the community.

Cravens remembered the rhetoric of that night as if it had happened last week.

"Jesus didn't come for the up and uppers. He came for the down and outers," one old disfigured woman, stooped over with her cane, had said. The walking skeleton of a person added: "And so help me, God, Howard Prickett is a savior in our community."

The council and the packed audience had roared their hearty affirmation, and the then wet-behind-the-ears journalist Jake Cravens shriveled in embarrassment. The result: The newspaper took a beating for crossing what many folks in in the community apparently thought was some sort of sacrosanct journalistic line—a case of "our town's paper gettin' above its raisin,'" as one inflamed citizen put it.

Howard Prickett, pictured on the front page of the *News-Journal* the next day with a big smile on his face—as if he were celebrating his vindication—kept his cozy, lucrative contract with the police and sheriff's departments. A contract that was his, without any additional challenges, until he died years later.

"And that's when I began learning about freedom of the press and the quest for truth in a small town, Mr. Lowery," Cravens said. "Sometimes Summer's Rest can't handle the truth or doesn't want the truth. Journalism in a small town is a different kettle of fish from journalism in a big city. It's more intimate, more personal. We all have to get along here in our little corner of East Tennessee. And I'd rather put a fire out with my newspaper than start one.

"You understand that, son?"

Stunned, the *News-Journal*'s young editor said nothing. Instead, he thought about why he was now where he was—at the top position in the newsroom of the town's only newspaper—and how he'd gotten there. Some of his mentors at the university where he'd earned his degree in journalism—and where he'd been the editor of the student newspaper—had warned him of the pluses and minuses of working on a small community paper. They had told him that there was no such thing as detachment or objectivity in newspapering in a small town, because you as a journalist were inescapably personally close to your readers and advertisers. You could never get around that. Never completely separate yourself—as a journalist—from the community you covered because you were not *apart from* the community but rather *a part of it*. As a consequence, they said, you'd have to tread very carefully on any potentially big story you decided to pursue. Because what you wrote didn't ever just alienate a few people. Your writing had the capacity to alienate the entire community and even to make you regret that you had ever decided to rock the boat.

But Dudley Lowery, idealist that he was, hadn't bought that. He had thought that people are people—everywhere. That they're the same in small towns as they are in big cities. And so it must be for journalism. Lowery was convinced that people, regardless of where they lived, cherished the truth. And that's what they wanted from their hometown newspaper—the truth.

After all, hadn't small town newspapers in North Carolina and Iowa in recent years won journalism's highest award—the Pulitizer Prize for Public Service? They'd risked upsetting the power structure and their readers and advertisers in their community—and it had gotten them big time accolades.

So why not in Summer's Rest with the *News-Journal*? What was Jake Cravens preaching to him? The gospel of treading softly with what you say or write in this cozy little southern Appalachian town because it might rile up a few of the wrong people? The editor wasn't buying it. But still, he said nothing—only nodding yes when Cravens asked him again—pointedly— if he understood what he'd just heard.

"Very good, young man," Cravens said as he clapped his hands together and lit yet another cigar. "Now we both are clear about where we stand and where this newspaper stands with respect, especially, to our esteemed high sheriff, Ethan Coffmann, and the difficult position he now finds himself in. "Has my editor just been edified? Have I made myself perfectly clear?"

Lowery, the pencil behind his left ear about to fall out when his head dropped, said only three words: "I get it."

Chapter 10
Another Victim

The priority call came into the sheriff's office bright and early Monday morning. "Sheriff, this is Constable Ted Hayes out on Ratty Branch Road. I'm afraid I've got some bad news for you, sir."

High Sheriff Ethan Coffmann braced himself for the worst, took a deep breath and cupped the phone a bit closer to his left ear. "Spill it, constable."

"Well, Sheriff, I was out on patrol this morning—you know, cruisin around the lake—and was drivin' by Mrs. Gracie Spencer's trailer and somethin' didn't seem quite right. She always lets her dog out to pee and poop and run around right after first light, and today I didn't see him.

"And then, I got ta lookin' a little closer. The winder' on her front door was broken and the flower pot on the porch rail was done knocked clean over and broke to pieces.

"I knowed right then somethin' weren't quite right."

An annoyed Coffmann pressed him: "Just get to the point, Ted."

"Well, I reckon 'bout then is when I ´cided to go inside and have a look see, just to make sure the widow woman was all right."

"And you found what exactly, Ted?" the exasperated sheriff asked.

"She was deader'n my ex-wife, Sheriff—cold as one of them big catfishes at the bottom of the lake—and they was blood on the mattress, like as if she'd tried fightin' whoever done this to her. And she was plum' nekkid layin' there on her bed. And the bed—wasn't no sheets or blankets on it. Not even a pillow case—jes like with Miz Haynes."

The sheriff listened to the rest of it—to how it appeared that whoever broke into Mrs. Spencer's trailer had pryed the front door knob off—probably in the middle of the night when she was asleep; to how Duke, her black lab mix, was barking and sniffing and whimpering about the trailer and seemed to be sensing that something was wrong; to how Mrs. Spencer had a devoted daughter who lived just down the road—but out of sight and out of earshot; and to how her church family and closest neighbors, who also lived in trailers on the other side of a nearby grove of trees—were sure to be devastated.

"Now hear me really good, Ted," the sheriff said. "I want you to stay right there at the scene—until me and my deputies and the coroner arrive. But do not go back inside that trailer. And don't let nobody else go inside till we get there. Nothing is to be disturbed. Not one iota, Ted. You understand?"

The high sheriff tried to be firm with the man on the other end of the phone without antagonizing him. He had always had a kind of love-hate relationship with the 16 constables of Taylor County. Accountable to no one—except for the voters who elected them—the constables tended to be ex-law enforcement officers who for whatever reason couldn't put that chapter of their life behind them when they retired. They patrolled the county—at their own expense in their own cars—writing traffic citations, making arrests and serving court summonses. Their pay came from a percentage of the court costs attached to each offense or summons.

As one of them had put it in a recent interview with the media, "We do our jobs as constables and pay our own expenses, because we like to catch bad guys and make a little money to boot. But we're really not in it for the money. We just want to make our communities safer places for all of us."

All that was well and good, but Coffmann had always thought of them as a kind of poor man's vigilante—out there patrolling the highways and by-ways of Taylor County for a rush of adrenalin and for a sense of self-worth—all while putting a modest sum of money in their pockets. He had learned to tread carefully with them and to treat them with respect, even though on occasion he thought they'd been overzealous in making an arrest or writing someone a driving citation.

Constable Ted Hayes, however, didn't fit the mold of a man who worked his job solely for money or excitement. For one thing, Hayes, a former deputy sheriff, had spent a good bit of his own commissions buying a police K-9 dog. For another, Hayes had a reputation for donating at least half of what he earned from his elected position to a local animal shelter.

"I understand, Sheriff. I ain't tamperin' with nothin' at that crime scene. Didn't touch a dad-gummed thing. I was learned right good, a long time ago in my trainin', about not disturbin' any prints or upsettin' any trace DNA evidence."

Coffmann doubted that Hayes even knew what trace DNA evidence was, but he let that one pass, telling the constable instead that he himself and several of his officers—along with the county coroner and an agent from the Tennessee Bureau of Investigation—would soon be on the scene.

"Just hold down the fort till we get there, Ted, and thanks for helping us with this. I know it's bad. Thanks for calling me right away. You've done the right thing."

In the background, as they spoke, the sheriff could hear the victim's dog barking and howling. The forlorn canine seemed to already be going through some serious withdrawal pains from losing its master. *If only that dog could talk,* the sheriff thought.

Thirty minutes later, the sheriff and two of his senior deputies arrived at the crime scene. Five minutes after that, the county coroner and a forensics expert from the Tennessee Bureau of Investigation also pulled up.

The first order of business was to secure the scene with yellow crime scene tape. The second was for all the officers to put on disposable blue plastic booties over their shoes. And the third was for all hands to be covered with black nitrile gloves.

"Men, we'd first like to thank constable Ted Hayes for everything he's already done. Constable Hayes was the first on the scene and he informs me that he has not touched or bothered anything inside the victim's trailer. So, Ted, a tip of our hats to you for all that you've already so carefully done."

Hayes, nodding slightly, grinned like a possum. "Sheriff, I'm honored to be of service in any way to the people of Taylor County. After all, that's my sworn duty as an elected constable."

Sheriff Coffmann said: "Gentlemen, I am the lead investigator on this case and so I will be the first one to go inside. Following my lead will be Mr. Fred Brown of the TBI and our county coroner, Mr. Jefferson Mills."

The sheriff pointed to the TBI representative, but he really didn't need to because the professorial-looking, short, bespectacled man wore a jacket with big bright yellow letters that proclaimed "Tennessee Bureau of Investigation."

As to the square jawed, balding, tall county corner—known around Taylor County as "a tall drink of water"— everyone already knew him from the many homicide and accidental death cases he had worked.

In fact, Jefferson Mills had been consumed by death all his life. As a student at Summer's Rest High School, he'd dug graves during the summer at Heaven's Valley Memorial Gardens. From there, after graduation, he'd joined the Air Force and been a mortuary technician at Dover Air Force Base—drop off point during the Vietnam War of the thousands of flag-draped coffins, with the bodies of U.S. troops, killed in Southeast Asia.

After his discharge from the military, Mills had stayed in the death business, working his way up from a mortuary assistant at the Hearts & Flowers Funeral Home in Summer's Rest to getting his degree in mortuary science and then rising to be director of the funeral home. His pedigree had also been death—his grandfather digging up many a corpse that had to be relocated before the nearby TVA lake was constructed in the late 1940s.

"Mr. Brown and I will be searching for clues to the identity of who committed this crime," the sheriff said. "We will be dusting for fingerprints, shoe impressions and combing the scene for hairs, fibers, body fluids, gunshot residue and the list goes on. You know the drill.

"While we conduct our walk through, the rest of you will do your utmost to make sure no unauthorized person gets past that yellow tape." The sheriff pointed to the tape—emblazoned with big black letters CRIME SCENE DO NOT CROSS—that enclosed Mrs. Spencer's trailer, porch and yard.

One of the deputies asked, "What about the press, sir? This dang thing's been all over our radios, and them newspaper guys monitor what we're sayin' 24 hours a day. Why, that editor man practically sleeps with his police scanner."

"I said *nobody* gets inside, and that's what I meant!" the sheriff declared. "I don't give a shit if he's from the New York Times. He's not contaminating my crime scene!"

"I gotcha sheriff," the deputy replied meekly.

With that, the sheriff, TBI investigator and county coroner set about the grisly but necessary task of taking a close look at the deceased, collecting what potentially could be forensic evidence left on her body by her assailant and taking pictures of her and the mattress she lay on from every conceivable angle.

"This woman's been strangled, Sheriff," the coroner said. "All the tell-tale signs are here—bruise marks and indentions on her neck, tiny busted blood vessels under her eyelids from her neck being squeezed so hard, red marks around her eyes which we call *petechiae.*

"And whoever did this to her, Sheriff, did it with his bare hands. He didn't cut off her air supply with a ligature."

"How you knowin' that?" the sheriff asked, a bit peeved that the coroner could be overreaching his bounds. Jefferson Mills was an elected official in Taylor County—well acquainted with suspicious deaths or obvious homicides—but he was not a physician or forensic pathologist. His central purpose, on being dispatched to a crime scene, was to certify that someone was dead and to pronounce—subject to change later by the medical examiner—the official date and time of death.

"Because I can flat out see where he wrapped his fingers around her scrawny little neck, Sheriff. Wrung her neck like it was a wet worsh' cloth. This man's big. He's strong. He's brutal. And five'll get you ten that he's left his fingerprints on her body. If not on her body, then somewhere else in this trailer. What I'm seein' here is a victim who was murdered by someone who flew into a rage. Who was so angry at whatever that I'm sure he got careless and has left something of hisself here."

The TBI forensics expert said he agreed that whoever committed the crime would almost certainly be caught because he noticed blood under Mrs. Spencer's fingernails.

The sheriff, nodding, said, "Let's get some paper bags over her hands just in case you're right and there's trace evidence under her fingernails."

"She put up a right good fight, Sheriff. She resisted. It was no use, but she tried, and he left a piece of himself under her fingernails. And once we get that to the lab and analyze it, I'm sure we'll have his DNA.

"He's mean. He's a killer and a rapist, and I'm sure he's done this before."

"So you sayin' she was sexually assaulted?" the sheriff asked.

Between snapping pictures, the TBI agent said, "I'd bet my life on it. Appears to me that he stripped her and forced her to have sex with him and then, figuring he wanted to leave a clean slate with no evidence, he strangled her. After that, he took her bedsheets, blankets and pillow cases. We'll know soon enough about whether she was in fact raped when the medical examiner takes a close look at her insides."

"Ok, get your iphone or tape recorder or whatever you have and say that again," the high sheriff ordered. "I want a record of everything we see here or even think we see. Don't worry about trying to sound pretty. At this point we just want your first impressions. The ME might find those very useful."

Neither Summer's Rest nor Taylor County had a full time medical examiner because they couldn't afford paying the $125,000 yearly salary for a licensed physician/forensic pathologist. That being the case, the county relied on the services of Dr. Kay Robinson, chief resident and board-certified forensic pathologist, to do autopsies in any high profile criminal investigation. When she wasn't conducting autopsies, she was a tenured faculty member at a respected medical school in East Tennessee.

"Doc Robinson'll do her thing, but I gar-an-tee you that I'm right on the money with how she died," the coroner said. "I don't need no fancy dancy, highfalutin medical examiner to tell me what I already know."

"I just need you to pronounce the woman dead, Jefferson," the sheriff said. "Can you do that?"

"She's deader'n a doornail, Sheriff. And I'd say she took her last breath about eight hours ago. I've got a body bag in the trunk of my car if you need one."

The sheriff thanked him for the gesture but said his deputies already had a body bag and that he could go ahead and leave.

The coroner tipped his ball cap—emblazoned in big yellow letters with COUNTY CORONER—then put his hands on his waist. "And one more thing, Sheriff. Her dog seen the whole thing. Hear that howlin'? That rascal's in mournin'. And if it were me, I'd take the dog, along with the victim's body, to Doc Robinson. You never know..."

Sheriff Coffmann thought at first that was a cockeyed idea, but *What could it hurt? Who knew what a dog could tell them—even if it couldn't speak human language?*

Chapter 11
Haunting Questions

A week later, the medical examiner's preliminary report arrived at the sheriff's office. Hair, blood, semen and fiber analysis was pending.

The report mainly detailed the cause of Gracie Spencer's death. But High Sheriff Ethan Coffmann didn't need an autopsy result to confirm what he already suspected. Both Hazel Eula Haynes and Gracie Spencer were clearly assaulted and murdered by the same man. Even without the forensic evidence from both murder scenes, the similarities between the murders were unmistakable. Both victims were elderly, frail women—utterly helpless to save themselves from such dark evil. They had both apparently tried to fight off their attacker—to no avail. They had both been overwhelmed by brute, physical force and had been strangled. Both lived in old trailers—not exactly fortresses of security. Both lived alone and could not have protected themselves with a firearm even if they'd wanted to. Reason being, they didn't own a gun, and, like so many other grandparents, most likely feared having a gun around their grandchildren or great grands. Both were sexually assaulted by a man intent on completely covering his tracks. In both instances, the perpetrator had bruised severely their internal private parts. Authorities found both women naked, with their bed clothing missing.

In both cases, money was likely not what the assailant was after. Both victims drove old cars and led meager life styles. Mrs. Haynes, whose only income was her monthly Social Security, had less than $75 cash in her trailer. Police knew she kept little cash—from interviews with her daughters, who visited their mother on a regular basis. Likewise, Mrs. Spencer, who also made ends meet with her monthly Social Security check, had only about $50 near her bedside on the last night of her life. Her daughter said she kept that in a locked box on her nightstand—saving it for her church.

On the other hand, both victims did indeed possess something that criminals in East Tennessee couldn't seem to get enough of—prescription opioid pills. Mrs. Haynes had been taking hydrocodone to help her deal with her rheumatoid arthritis, but she happened not to have had any on the night she was murdered. Mrs. Spencer kept her excruciating back and left hip pains at bay by taking a daily dose of oxycodone.

So both had been taking helpful but potentially dangerous prescription medications. Helpful because the medicines gave them at least temporary relief from excruciating pain. Dangerous because opioids had fast begun replacing methamphetamine as the drugs of choice for criminals out to make a fast buck in the mountains of East Tennessee.

A criminal could steal tablets of oxycodone, for example, cut them into halves or even fourths and sell them on the street—or even to seniors in public housing—at a premium price.

Coffmann read the medical examiner's report carefully, then re-read it. It posed more questions than answers. Who, for example, would target old practically penniless women for their drugs? And who would mercilessly rape such completely helpless, feeble victims? And what of strangling them? What did that tell you about the murderer? Was he someone with a criminal record who could not pass a background check to buy a gun? Wouldn't a knife have served him more quickly and easily? Did he get his kicks out of physically overpowering his prey with his bare hands? And what of taking the nightgowns, bedsheets, blankets and pillow cases? Did the perpetrator figure that was part of covering his tracks—removing any vestiges of his DNA? If so, had DNA left at a crime scene done him in previously? Could his DNA be on record in a national DNA database?

The medical examiner's report also mentioned Duke, Mrs. Spencer's dog. The canine had yelped, as if in pain, when a deputy sheriff had tried to handle it. A veterinarian x-rayed its front and hind legs and had detected that someone had kicked the dog forcefully—not once but several times. The doctor said it was impossible to know for sure what exactly had caused the bone damage, but he theorized that someone with work boots had kicked Duke repeatedly.

Coffmann recalled the coroner's parting words to him: *Her dog seen the whole thing. Hear that howlin'? That rascal's in mournin'.*

But the droopy-eyed dog, howling and barking, had not just been grieving the death of its owner. Someone had injured it. Either stomped it or kicked it. Duke had been in severe pain. He put the medical examiner's report in the top drawer of his desk when someone rapped loudly on his office door.

It was Roby Cooper, his chief deputy. He had a buzz cut, a slicked down mustache and long sideburns, and his uniform shirt, as always, was clean and starched. He also had, as did all the other deputies in the sheriff's department, the same sidearm, a 9 millimeter Glock 17 handgun, in his holster. In addition—"just in case," as Cooper put it—the chief deputy kept a Glock 43 9 millimeter revolver strapped to his other side.

"Sheriff, I hate to tell you this, but we've gotta a big problem on our hands. Another one of our deputies has gotten his nuts in a vice."

"Spill it, Deputy Cooper. And don't tell me I've got yet another messy personnel scandal to deal with in my department." The sheriff looked at Cooper menacingly. He had never personally liked him, but his highest ranked deputy had risen to his position because he'd long been a good cop with the city before signing on with the sheriff's department. Coffmann remembered Cooper telling him that he hadn't gotten the respect that he thought he deserved as a police officer patrolling the town's city limits. Around town, he'd made some folks angry because, to their mind, he wrote far too many speeding tickets. He had heard all their lame excuses when he pulled out his ticket pad—including, 'Officer, gimme a break. I gotta get home cause I got a cake'a cornbread in the oven and it's burnin'. Or, "Officer, my wife's done gone into labor and the am-bu-LANCE is rushin' her to the hospital. I've got ta' get there to hold her hand.' But no matter what they came up with, Cooper would just keep writing and hand them that despised piece of paper.

"Do you know what it takes to be a cop in Summer's Rest?" Cooper recalled one of his cousins noting sarcastically. "Three-hundred and fifty dollars a week and a son-of-a-bitch."

That had stuck with the surprisingly sensitive, image-conscious police officer, hurting him deeply. And so, when a position—and a slightly higher paying one at that—had become available with the county sheriff's department, Cooper had eagerly jumped ship.

"I don't know how to say this, so I'll just come right to it. One of our deputies has been a bad egg. As my blessed momma—God rest her soul—used to tell me, he just needs to grease his feet and go to bed.

Another reason Coffmann disliked his chief deputy: *The man talked ad nauseum in riddles.*

The sheriff said nothing, just pausing and bracing to listen to whatever bad news Cooper was about to lay on him.

"Sheriff, there just ain't no other way to put it: Deputy Bruce Jones frisked a female a little too much when he pulled her over for speeding about three miles out of town. And now that woman has gotten her little fanny a lawyer and guess what? We're being sued!"

"On what grounds exactly?" the sheriff asked. He was getting more upset by the second. Jones had a reputation for ogling women and bragged about his sexual conquests. But Coffmann had always thought he was just full of hot air.

"She's claimin' defecation of char-act-ter and sexual har-rass-ment, Sheriff. Says our deputy done flicked his tongue and brushed her breast with his hand when he handed her license back to her."

Unhappy as he was, Coffmann couldn't help but smirk. "Ok, Cooper. So what, exactly, do you recommend we do with Deputy Jones?"

What is happening to this world? Coffmann thought. Women were yelling sexual harassment at every turn. With Bill O'Reilly at Fox News. With some bigshot movie man Harvey Weinstein. With Charlie Rose at NBC. With Matt Laurer at ABC. With some judge running for U.S. senator in Alabama. With an 88-year-old congressman in Michigan. With a U.S. senator in Minnesota. With nationally admired Garrison Keillor of public radio. With acclaimed talk show host Tavis Smiley. With a doctor up north who'd taken serious liberties with young Olympic gymnasts on his examining table. Even Bill Cosby, once thought of as "America's Dad," had found himself in deep legal doo-doo for allegedly drugging women and taking advantage of them. *Whatever happened to just flirting with a woman?*

All had been cast as sexual predators. Their careers and lives had been ruined—even if they somehow might later be exonerated. Coffmann had heard a curious term—toxic masculinity—on a cable news show that previous night. And now, toxic masculinity, whatever that meant, seemed to be on the verge of hurting the Taylor County Sheriff's Department.

"Ain't nothin' to do but suspend him without pay," Cooper opined. "And just between you and me, I knowed he was no count when I first met him."

"How's that, Cooper?"

"Just a feelin' I had, Sheriff. I cain't rightly put it into words."

"Okay, Deputy Cooper. I'll take this whole matter under advisement and take the appropriate action. Meanwhile, as far as I'm concerned, someone ought to really know what they become if they sue us.

"What's that, sir?" Cooper asked.

"Ask 'em if they really want to be a sewer."

Cooper laughed and left Coffmann's office.

Later that same day, in consultation with the Tennessee Burea of Investigation, the high sheriff of Taylor County read over a press release. It contained a profile of the person or persons law enforcement sought in connection with the murders of Hazel Eula Haynes and Gracie Spencer. It also asked for the public's help. The sheriff understood that publication of a composite profile was potentially risky. For one thing, it might open a floodgate of useless information, much of it nonetheless having to be checked out. That would do nothing but stretch his beleaguered department's already thin resources. For another, such a profile might tend to incriminate some innocent people. Tongues wagged and fingers pointed quickly in a small town, and no one was immune from being incorrectly and unnecessarily defamed.

Regardless of the potential drawbacks, the sheriff decided to go ahead with making the press release public. Who knew, after all, where it might lead authorities in their thus-far-fruitless-dead-end hunt for the murderer?

He called his clerk into his office. “Get Jake Cravens and his editor Dudley Lowery over here right away. Tell ’em there’s been a development in the two murder cases.”

The shapely clerk, dying to know what her boss was about to announce, nevertheless kept respectfully silent. She nodded, moved a strand of her thick lustrous brown hair out of her sparkling green eyes and left.

Coffmann reminded himself to somehow let her know that she was to begin dressing more professionally. To especially wear skirts that weren’t so tight or silky see-through blouses that showed more than they concealed. *All I need, on top of everything else, is a charge of toxic masculinity from my own clerk,* he mused uneasily.

When publisher Cravens burst into his editor’s office, ordering him to put his shirt tail in and try to look more professional, a haggard Dudley Lowery glanced up from his computer and said, “What’s up, boss? I’m on deadline.”

“You work for me, Mr. Lowery, and you’ll do as I say!” Cravens shot back. “Now get your reporter’s notebook and your iphone or whatever it is that you’re always checking and come along with me. I’ve got a feelin’ that we’re about to get our lead story for tomorrow’s edition from Sheriff Coffmann. And I’m not talkin’ ’bout some fluff piece about how he keeps his jail clean.”

Lowery sensed that his boss, who absolutely loved hard news—and the more negative the news was the better—was practically salivating. He’d heard the publisher bark many times, “Good news is no news! Give me some good ole blood’n guts. That’s what sells newspapers!”

The old school publisher of the *News-Journal* was right from purely an economic standpoint. The editor had seen for himself that when the paper led on the front page with a murder, assault or big drug bust, counter sales of the *News-Journal* spiked. Folks could complain till the cows came home about how the press was infatuated with negative news—journalism that served up an overly bleak, dark portrait of reality. But at their core, people were hard wired to learn about that bleakness. Such news was what fed the local gossip mills—whether it was people talking while in line at the funeral home or while they slurped their morning coffee at McDonald's or were getting their hair done at salons or barber shops.

And if it were hard news emanating from the Taylor County Sheriff's Office or from the Summer's Rest Police Department, all the better—as far as the publisher of the *News-Journal* was concerned. That's because such news was coming from an official source and tended to be the kind of journalism backed up with court or law enforcement documents. Documents that were public record and therefore containing content that was virtually immune from being the target of a successful libel suit.

Safe but explosive, tantalizing journalism—exactly what made Jake Cravens' day.

"Now, Jake, I'm just gonna say this one more time," an increasingly irritated Sheriff Coffmann admonished his close friend. "I'm going out on a limb to give you this press release as an exclusive, and so the Tennessee Bureau of Investigation and the Taylor County Sheriff's Department expects you to run it verbatim. No editing or changing even one word, Jake. You have to promise me that."

Cravens and his editor had already read the three-paragraph press release and spoke eagerly in front of the sheriff about how they might "play" it in the *News-Journal*. "I want you to jazz this up and add some color. Make it sizzle. I don't care how you do it. Just do it!" Cravens had said excitedly to Lowery.

But such talk made the high sheriff nervous. The last thing he wanted was for the local newspaper to hurt his investigation.

At that moment, the sheriff's desk clerk, who'd had her left ear pressed against her boss' door the entire time, buzzed him. "Sheriff Coffmann, there's a group of women here from Hazel Eula Haynes' and Gracie Spencer's churches. They say both Miz Hazel and Gracie were in their Sunday School classes. And they have a sum of money—reward money, they're calling it—that they'd like offer to help catch the murderer."

When the sheriff learned that the ladies had collected $1,000, he smiled and told his clerk to send them in. "Now Jake and Mr. Lowery, I'm not required to do this, but I'm giving you another exclusive. But before I do that, you have to give me your solemn promise you won't change that press release."

When the two newspaper men reluctantly nodded their acquiescence, the church ladies were ushered into the sheriff's office. One of them—dressed in her best with a red, wool felt floral hat, a button-front long polka-dotted dress and high heels—proudly opened a cloth-covered sewing box full of small bills—ones, fives, tens, twenties.

Mrs. Goody Two Shoes, Cravens thought.

"We had been collectin' this to help the young unmarried girls in our community whose baby-daddies weren't doing anything for them," she said, tugging at an annoying bra strap that kept wanting to inch down to the top part of her arm. "But we've decided that we want to help catch whoever it was that killed two of our own. So, Sheriff, on behalf of Ladies' Sunday School classes of the First Christian Church of Summer's Rest and the Lower Springs Baptist Church of Crescent Holler Road, we want to present you with this reward money."

"And are y'all the news men we've seen out and about?" asked another member of the group, smiling and pointing to Cravens and Lowery. She leaned forward slightly and her eyes seemed to widen.

When the two allowed that that's who they were, at least two of the churchgoers started fussing with their hair, wetting their lips and straightening their clothes.

Meanwhile, editor Lowery reminded himself to look up the meaning of the word "babydaddy." He'd learn later that a babydaddy was the father of a baby but was not the husband of the mother of that child.

"Now, oh dear, we didn't 'spect to get our pictures in the paper," one of church ladies said demurely. "But if you must …" She fiddled with her hair.

Chapter 12
The Coma Dream

It had been a full day for Taylor County High Sheriff Ethan Coffmann. The usual number of fender-benders at the busy intersection just outside Walmart.

Three teachers' cars reported keyed at the parking lot of the high school. An anonymous caller saying he'd seen a man siphoning off electrical power from his neighbor who apparently hadn't noticed, in plain daylight, the bright red extension cord between the two residences. A woman complaining that she was too old and frail and hard of hearing and seeing to visit her jailed son via video and wondering "why the heck cain't I go see him in person like they allow in any civilized jail?" Two calls from women who complained bitterly that their ex-husbands or boyfriends had violated orders of protection. A teenager caught making meth in the back seat of his dad's car—which he'd made off with while his old man, who worked graveyard shift, was fast asleep. Two requests for sheriff's deputies to escort mentally ill patients from the hospital in Summer's Rest to a psychiatric facility 15 miles away. These requests Sheriff Coffmann only grudgingly complied with because they were a drain on his department's resources, and, on occasion, the angry, upset passengers had been known to kick out the windows of the back of his squad cars.

And last, but not least, there had been a "break"—sort of—in the murders of the two elderly women. Still no solid leads but the local press would soon be publishing a profile description of the man so desperately being sought by law enforcement.

Coffmann hoped someone would come forward who had seen such a man. After all, the Summer's Rest-Taylor County community was small. And almost everyone seemed to be connected—in one way or another. You were either related to someone else or you knew someone who knew that person or knew of them.

And so where was this detached, quiet loner? This white, muscular man in his late 20s or 30s? A person who kept to himself and had few if any friends? A man, too, who probably was an "outsider," meaning he had moved in to the community from somewhere else. And a man, according to the profile that was soon to be published in the *News-Journal*, who likely wore scruffy clothes and boots and did odd jobs in construction or home repair. The profile description even had him with rough, calloused hands, scraggly, greasy hair, bad teeth, unshaven to help disguise himself—and driving an old beat up car or pickup truck.

Coffmann got in his sheriff's patrol car and began driving slowly—not to anywhere in particular but just to give himself time to think. Away from the pressures of his office. Away from those naysayers who surely, he believed, were circling him like vultures eager to end his career in law enforcement and to peck his heart and soul to pieces.

For the community he served, despite its facade of friendliness and Christian warmth, could also be cold and cruel. With two unsolved murders scaring the likes of even the most well-armed citizens, the town had turned inward against itself and the outside world. Many residents now fervently believed that no one was truly safe.

Coffmann mosied along in his squad car alongside the river that flowed majestically under the Covered Bridge and bisected Summer's Rest. Today, a cold fog rose up from the surface of the water. On the river's rocky banks were drooping branches of waxy-leafed mountain laurel. A long-beaked water bird, possibly a blue heron, waded among the rocks and vegetation. And there, at the river's edge, was an old bent-over woman wearing a shapeless winter coat. *Picked it up at Walmart or at a thrift store*, Coffmann surmised.

With her hair tied tightly back in a bun, she puffed on a cigarette, all the while not taking her stern eyes off the sheriff's car as he drove by her. To a stranger, she might have been homeless or forsaken by her family. Or an outcast. Or a prickly someone who just liked being left alone. But Sheriff Coffmann wasn't a stranger to the woman. They knew each other from her being in his jail for shoplifting at Walmart. She had stuffed a few candy bars into her baggy pants pockets. An overzealous security guard had nabbed her in the parking lot and next thing she knew she was in a jail cell. But not for long. The sheriff had personally intervened in the case, asking the manager of Walmart to drop the charges and give the petty thief another chance. He had and the woman had walked.

Coffmann waved to her but she paid him no mind. Instead, she abruptly turned away from him, flicked her cigarette butt to the ground and made her way toward Main Street in town. As she walked, she kept her head down—as if sending a signal that she wanted no company.

So he kept plodding along in his police cruiser—heading down Main Street. Christmas decorations—wreaths, lights and brightly colored ornaments—hung from the storefronts. Big brilliant, glowing stars, placed in honor of people who had recently died, hung from a few of the light poles. Children wandered rambunctiously down the sidewalks, their parents seemingly transfixed by their window shopping. With December 25th being just a few weeks away, Coffmann reminded himself to get something extra special for his wife Laura. *After all,* he thought, *she'd put up with a lot these last few weeks.* And she'd done it cheerfully, never letting on how she might have feared that her husband would soon be unemployed or even run out of town.

Now in their 30th year of marriage, they had been high school sweethearts—he voted as most athletic and she getting the nod as most attractive. They hadn't been able to stay away from each other. Where you saw Ethan, there, too, was Laura. They became not just steady in-love girlfriend and boyfriend—she with his ring on a gold chain around her neck and he with her pictures everywhere. They'd also turned into inseparable soulmates. And so, when Laura went off to college and Ethan joined the Marine Corps, they stayed in touch with each other every day.

It had been a hot but also tender and intimate romance for those years Laura worked on her teaching degree at the nearby university.

As for Ethan, he served his country honorably, achieving the Marine Corps' highest rank as an enlisted man. He also earned a Purple Heart for being wounded in Iraq and a commendation for surviving as a prisoner of war. He had come home to Summer's Rest to a hero's welcome—the town even making him grand marshal in the annual Thanksgiving parade—and to the loving, open, waiting arms of Laura. They had gotten married and Laura, fresh out of college with her teaching certificate, had gotten hired by Summer's Rest High School—where she retired and where even today, she still worked part-time and as a volunteer. Coffmann, meanwhile, had gotten on with the local police department, where he had almost immediately earned plaudits from his superiors and where the press regularly spotlighted his good deeds to the community. One thing had led to another, and here he was today: the high but now embattled sheriff of Taylor County, Tennessee.

Coffmann's radio crackled loudly.

"Sheriff Coffmann here," he said, holding down the button to the phone speaker. He turned the volume all the way up.

"Sheriff, what's your ten-twenty?" the dispatcher asked.

"I'm in front of the First National Bank," Hoffman answered. "Whaddya got?" What seemed liked minutes were only a few torturous seconds as the sheriff nervously waited for an answer. He glared at the sign on the bank—one he'd seen thousands of times while patrolling downtown. "Neighborly Service Since 1902," it proclaimed.

"We've got a possible one-eighty-seven on South Lestertown Road. Officers en route, sir."

Coffmann flipped on his siren and blue lights and pressed down on the accelerator as he got the specific address. The specially equipped 365-horsepower, V-6 Ford Crown Victoria Police Interceptor responded instantly. With over 300 foot-pounds of torque the car could reach top speed of 150 miles per hour in only a few seconds.

But the high sheriff also realized that he had to be extra careful—what with the nearby unpredictable children and their lollygagging, distracted parents. He looked both ways hurriedly and glanced in his rearview mirror. No one in sight.

So he floored it, and the Crown Vic roared to life. Lights flashing and siren blaring, Coffmann bolted out of town toward the location he had been dispatched to.

Always, when he got such a call, a rush of adrenalin coursed through his body. His hands and forehead began sweating and his heartbeat quickened.

Coffmann estimated he'd be there, contingent on traffic and drivers pulling over to the side of the road when they heard or saw him coming, in 15 minutes. But sometimes, the unpredictable would happen—a tractor or combine or hay baler driven by someone who either couldn't hear a siren or see a flashing police light—or who was just plain contrary and wouldn't pull over. Or a rutting buck could suddenly dash out from the woods along the road's edge and crash head-first, with his antlers, into your car. The sheriff hoped that today wasn't one of those days.

By the time Coffmann got to his destination, 133 South Lestertown Road, the driveway to that mobile home residence was a beehive of law enforcement and first responder activity. Several of his deputies, including Roby Cooper, were in the process of cordoning off the area with DO NOT CROSS, CRIME AREA police tape. Police K-9s, their heads down close to the ground and their tails wagging, were sniffing about the premises. Three state troopers, their hands on their hips and their wide brimmed mountie-type hats pulled down to their sunglass covered eyes, stood there as if keeping a vigil. Paramedics had just stepped out of an ambulance. One of them had what appeared to be a large jump bag—possibly packed with medications, bandages, and surgical supplies. Another carried a trauma/spinal board, and a third paramedic had an oxygen tank and defibrillator. They moved quickly and precisely.

The troopers dispersed, as best they could, a steadily growing, uneasy crowd of curiosity-seeking, picture-taking gawkers.

"Now, folks, this is a crime scene, and you best just be going along your way so we can do our job!" one of the troopers commanded.

"We ain't goin' nowheres!" one obstinate character in the crowd responded. "Cause we're payin' your salaries and we's got as much right to be here as you do!" The belligerent fellow had tattoos from his wrists up to his elbows. He wore a black wife beater tank shirt with the white initials "NRA" over his heart.

"And far as we're concerned," a woman in curlers, a robe and flip flops shouted from the mass of onlookers, "you can just git your own hind ends home!" She stood there, hands on her hips and craning her neck, like some sort of immovable object.

"Quit tryin' ta treat us like the poor relations!" still another woman demanded. "We're stayin' right here." She was braless under a too-snug faded purple sweater that clung to her huge sagging breasts.

"Deputy Cooper, what we got goin' on here?" Coffmann asked his top assistant.

"Her name was Carrie Belle Harris," Cooper said. "Neighbor from down the road a piece had called to check on her a couple of hours ago but she didn't answer. So she paid Carrie Belle a visit. Knocked on her door and 'cided somethin' weren't quite right, cause she didn't answer, and there her car was, biggern' life, in her driveway. So the neighbor cracked the door and yelled for her but Carrie Belle didn't come, and that's when she called us."

Coffmann asked his full-of-himself, ambitious deputy who had been inside the trailer. Cooper said no one, except for the inquiring neighbor who had told police that she had tiptoed back to Carrie Belle's bedroom and discovered her, eyes still wide open and her hands clutched in fists, stone cold dead.

"And then she said she screamed bloody murder and called us, right then and there, on her cell phone," the deputy said. "Said she didn't touch a blessed thing. So the crime scene should be exact, sir."

"Don't you mean intact, Deputy Cooper?"

"Uh, yes siree. That's what I meant to say. She GAR-an-teed me that she didn't touch a blamed thing inside that trailer."

"Okay, Deputy Cooper. You help control this crowd out here. I'm going inside. Absolutely no one, except for the boys from the Tennessee Bureau of Investigation and the county coroner is to be allowed inside this trailer. Understand?"

When Cooper said that he did, Taylor County's high sheriff put on his crime scene gloves and booties and stepped gingerly inside.

The first thing that caught his attention were toys—dolls and a doll house, little cars and trucks, Lincoln logs, blocks, guns and holsters, little girl makeup kits. The living room and leading into the hall were strewn with things that would keep little children—probably Carrie Belle's grandkids, Coffmann thought—entertained and busy.

Next to stand out to the high sheriff were the many framed family pictures placed on almost every item of furniture—on the coffee table, the end tables, the space on both sides of the flat screen TV on the entertainment center, in the middle of the dining room table. Pictures of family members and friends also lined the paneled walls of the trailer—starting in the living room and running the down the hall and into the bedroom. A framed embroidered Bible verse hanging on the wall above her bed read: "Yea, though I walk through the valley of the shadow of death, I will fear no evil, for Thou art with me …"

A basket on a bedroom nightstand—the sort of sweet-grass woven basket that you would buy from one of those Gullah women in the Low Country of South Carolina—was where Carrie Belle had apparently kept her medications. There were lots of medicine bottles in it, but all of them were empty.

And there on the bed, which had been stripped of its sheets, blankets and pillow cases, was the bloodied and bruised lifeless body of Carrie Belle Harris. She was naked with black and blue marks on the inside of her thighs and around her genitalia. A tiny silver cross on a delicate gold chain still hung around her neck. According to a card on an end table on the other side of her bed, she had just celebrated her 83rd birthday.

Coffmann took a close look at the birthday greeting. It bore the signatures of about 12 people—undoubtedly belonging to Carrie Belle's children and grandchildren.

Next to the birthday card was a crinkled and smudged church bulletin—the inside of it full of someone's scribblings. Probably put there by Carrie Belle as she took notes of the Sunday church sermon. A page in the church bulletin listed "Sick and Shut-ins." Some of the names on that list had been circled.

And then, without touching the corpse, Hoffman examined it. Evidence of strangulation—from the bruises on her neck. Evidence, too, that the victim hadn't succumbed easily. Because the high sheriff was certain that the murderer had unwillingly left something of himself under her fingernails. She had clawed and scratched and writhed and punched, as best she could—all of it useless. Because the animal who did this to her had been too big, too strong, too vicious.

The same calling card as with his first two victims, Coffmann thought. *And so now he's had his way with three old women. And he's still out there, roaming around, waiting for his next prey. Maybe even stalking that prey.*

Exasperated and angry, the high sheriff had seen enough.

"Somebody call the medical examiner!" he commanded. "And where the hell is the Tennessee Bureau of Investigation?!"

Deputy Cooper assured him that TBI agents were on their way.

"Why don't you go on home, sir? Me and the other deputies and the dogs have got this under control. The coroner will be here any minute. And we'll be damned sure you won't have to lick this calf over."

That night, the embattled chief law enforcement officer of Taylor County, Tennessee, downed four shots of Jack Daniels whiskey. Straight. On ice. And then he practically staggered in a daze to the guest bedroom. For Laura didn't like him sleeping with her in such a state. And she was angry, though she tried not to show it, for what her husband was going though.

She despised the threats and finger-pointing from the once supportive community. And there was the increasing widespread public fear that what had already happened to three old women would soon claim a fourth woman and maybe a fifth and then on and on.

She was also keenly aware of the whispers from even among the sheriff's most ardent supporters and close friends that his best days of upholding the law were behind him.

So tonight, she decided that it was best that her husband sleep alone. For they had been through such trying times before—though not nearly this bad. They had always stood their ground and come out of a crisis stronger and closer and more determined than ever to make the most of their intertwined lives.

The whiskey that he drank that night had the desired effect. It numbed him. Helped him forget what challenges he would face the next day. Made him sleepy and then he found himself in what he would later describe to Laura as a "coma dream."

It was a kind of gauzy, faraway, surrealistic world where Ethan Coffmann was totally at ease with himself. Where no one could hurt him or any member of his family. Where everything and every person was fuzzy and yet so very real. Where there, before his very eyes, he witnessed the murders of Hazel Eula Haynes, Gracie Spencer and Carrie Belle Harris.

Only he couldn't quite see the murderer clearly. It was more like watching him move about teasingly through a fog.

Some aspects of his features, however, he could make out. The guy was big—really big. With bulging biceps that stretched his t-shirt, he could have been a champion weightlifter.

The high sheriff knew what big was because he himself stood a towering six and a half feet tall and weighed a tad over 240 pounds.

And the man who killed the three church-going women wore a ball cap. On backwards. Like one of those young guys on a baseball team who liked to cut up, make jokes and have fun.

He was white and broad shouldered and had beefy hands with dirty fingernails. Someone who you wouldn't want to take on in a street fight. And he laughed, yes laughed raucously, when his victims took their last breaths. Seemed to get his jollies from seeing them die.

In his coma dream, Ethan Coffmann tried to apprehend the murderer. Tried to stop him from killing. But the sheriff was locked in some sort of cage—helpless to stop anything from happening—and he smelled of ink, like what he'd smelled coming out of the basement of the building that housed Jake Cravens' press. It was as if the community that had elected him to "protect and serve" had decided he was no longer one of the good guys. Had lumped him in, somehow, with a newspaper that they'd come to despise on too many occasions.

All he could do was watch. Watch agonizingly while the public ridiculed him and spat on him. Watch while the town's alternately liked and disliked newspaper, the *News-Journal*—ran full page venomous ads, placed by so called "concerned citizens," against him.

And, in his coma dream, he could also hear. He could hear the screaming and pleading of the victims.

And then he heard a loud YELP! Like you'd hear when a dog gets hurt and needs attention. The black lab mix. He could see it clearly. Even when he couldn't quite make out the blurry, distorted, crazed face of the man who injured the animal.

The man swatted at the dog with his huge hands. He missed. The dog kept growling and barking and pawing.

And then the enraged criminal had at the dog with his left foot. Except the man's foot wasn't bare. What he had on, Coffmann couldn't tell, but it was some kind of hightop laceup shoe. Covered in mud and grime. Or maybe it was a boot he tried to kick the dog with?

When he woke up, hours later, High Sheriff Ethan Coffman would recall little of what he had dreamed. But there had been something—in that coma dream—about a dog. A dog so real and alive, in the sheriff's brain, that he must have dreamed about it for a reason.

"Honey, did you get some sleep last night?" Laura asked him. She looked as pretty as ever. She had brought him a cup of hot coffee and two lemon filled doughnuts (his favorites).

After he wiped the sleep out of his eyes, the two hugged and kissed sweetly, and they promised each other that everything would be okay.

If only I could remember more from that dream, he thought. What stood out to him was the dog. But what did that mean? The dog had somehow helped open up a gateway to his subconscious. Helped him picture, in that subconscious, the man who was causing so much death and fear. But now, because the dream had seemed to dissipate like a morning fog, he could no longer recall—with the exception of the dog—what had seemed so real as he slept.

Chapter 13

Staying Clear of the Law

It was a cold, sunny afternoon in the dark remote woods where David Patrick Jackson III lay half asleep.

Humming birds fluttered quietly just outside the duck taped cracked window in the bedroom of his ancient, decrepit trailer. Some of the tiny mountain birds had red-orange bills. But Jackson's favorites were the ones with dark green and metallic blue all over their heads or breasts.

He slowly rose, stretched and made his way to the outside toilet. No need to get dressed because no other human being lived within sight.

After completing his business in the outhouse, he took a quick look around his premises. A bushy-tailed squirrel scampered up a big oak tree, and he could hear the cawing of a crow in the distance. But there was no sign of anything disturbed. And not even the slightest hint that another person had ventured to his little private abode in this thick wooded terrain.

Just the way David Patrick Jackson III liked it.

But he knew if he stayed here much longer, someone was bound to stumble upon him. Some nosey hiker or bird watcher or, heaven forbid, a ranger, police officer or game warden. And if that happened, he'd be in deep shit.

Jackson began hatching a plan. A plan to stop his world from spinning out of control.

The first order of business: hide any papers that he'd been given from the parole board when he got out of prison. Stuff all those documents in a big jar and bury them, along with any opioids he had gotten from his prey.

Do all that just to be on the safe side. Because if the police all of a sudden busted into his place he didn't want to give them even a scent of an idea that he could have killed those three old women.

By all means, bury them papers where they couldn't be found, even by smart-sniffin' dogs. Then find a place to hide his drugs to keep them dry so that he'd be able to retrieve them when he needed a "high" to get through the day. Yep, dang right that's what David Patrick Jackson III decided he'd do. He slept peacefully with his little pills, but was always looking over his shoulders. So play it safe. Gather up all those precious little bottles of oxycodone, hydrocodone, Demerol and Percocet and his homemade Meth and stuff 'em, he told himself, "where the sun don't shine."

But then he had another problem. Even if "they"—whoever "they" might happen to be—couldn't connect him to those opioids, there was the situation with that damned profile description published in the local newspaper.

How to remedy that? Not a problem for the cunning "old knife and chisel man" who was determined never again to serve another day in a stinkin' prison.

He hadn't even personally read that profile description. Hell, he had never read a newspaper in his life! But he had overheard a couple of old snuff-chewing geezers jabbering about it at a local cafe. And one thing that he remembered was that the suspect police sought was a big, bulky man.

Well, nothing could be much more common in the mountains of east Tennessee than "big bulky guys." Anyway, he would stay away from crowds. Keep out of the public eye. *Don't let old nosey rosey finger me!*

He'd also overheard the old men say the killer probably had a beard. Problem solved just as quick as you please with a razor blade and shaving cream.

Jackson gazed at his now-smooth face in the cloudy, spotted mirror on the wall of his cabin. He primped. Turned this way and that. Grinned, smacked his lips and batted his eyes. *Ain't half bad. Why, I might even like this town so good, that I might oughta stick around a while longer. Maybe find me a little darlin' and bring her to my love shack.*

He knew that was foolish, but it was fun to imagine that once again he'd be with a woman the way a man should be. Not by forcing them to do anything, let alone "the deed"—against their will. And not by squeezing the life out of them.

No, not that way.

Many years ago—before he'd been sentenced to pull time in that awful state prison in West Tabor City, N.C.—he'd had a gal friend. And he'd learned from her that a woman likes to be treated gentle—like cuddling with a little kitten.

Her name was Sonja Powers. And he and Sonja, who was slender and biracial and had the prettiest brown eyes you ever saw, had grown to like each other very much. They had met, innocently enough in an elevator at a national trade conference once upon a time a long time ago (it now seemed to him) when he had a real professional job. She had worked for the competition, but that made no difference to David, because from very quickly he could tell she was a smart, creative woman.

But it was Sonja's looks that first got his attention. She had been a definite head turner.

Never, ever would David forget his first brush with her in that elevator.

Her white gold earrings and matching necklace had shone alluringly, dangling over just a hint of tempting cleavage. And her skirt had clung ever so close to her hips—as if her body had been poured into it.

But if she'd wanted to just give him a "hint" of her assets (and nothing more) the young woman with so much magnetism had failed. Because David's brain couldn't help but imagine what was beneath that blouse. And when she bent over, ever so slightly and teasingly, to scratch her left knee, what a view!

When she rose up and in one motion with her bejeweled fingers straightened her skirt, which ended temptingly about two inches above her knees, he knew he shouldn't be staring.

He had felt more than a twinge of guilt and embarrassment, along with a surge of excitement, but Sonja Powers had just laughed—seemingly enjoying his awkwardness. Then she had winked and smiled at him and introduced herself—extending a meaningful, heartfelt handshake, not just a perfunctory "Glad to meet you" greeting. And through it all she had grinned, licked her lips with a heavenly tongue and played with the top button of her blouse.

She had for sure known that his eyes had been locked on hers, and when it had come time to leave the elevator, they both happily discovered they had adjoining rooms on the same floor.

And Sonja Powers had heartily laughed at that, too.

Even today, David Jackson III remembered her exact precise words as she had grabbed hold of his hand, looked him straight in the eye and declared: "Look at us! We are too good, too serious! Swallowed up by our work. Who do we think we are?! Nobody's that important. You'd think we already owned our gosh-darned companies. Why don't we celebrate by having dinner and wine together and watching an in-room movie?"

Not believing the invitation he'd just heard, David had asked her if she had a boyfriend. Without hesitating, she had told him she was married but that her husband was disabled and she'd tell him all about it later.

So that was the beginning of an erotic, fun evening he'd remember for the rest of his life. And it was the start of a pleasurable, loving relationship that would last for many months—with Sonja's husband getting worse, it seemed, by the day.

Oh, the memories that he cherished with them together.

He laughed now when he harkened back to that hot muggy summer night when he'd taken her—in his vintage 1965 Chevy Corvette—to the Dairy Queen in her hometown of Belmont, North Carolina.

They had both been standing in line on that hot, muggy night—the supposedly open-minded couples in that line trying not to stare at the beautiful light skinned woman.

The server, a short jowly woman, had been behind the window of the DQ scooping ice cream.

"Where's Kenny?!" a woman in her twenties, waiting in line, had called out to the ice cream scooping employee, layers of fat sagging from her waistline.

"Kenny ain't here!" she replied. "He done drunk hisself to Bolivia!"

David and Sonja had laughed so hard that they thought they were making a scene. But everyone else had either missed that comment, or, if they'd heard it, had apparently paid it no mind. Just the way salt of the earth folks talked in Belmont, David figured.

And there was the time when she'd shared with him that she felt totally safe and comfortable with a white man—as opposed to some of the black boyfriends she'd had in her younger years.

"But they can jump higher and run faster than me. And they're stronger," he'd said. "I'm just a slow, weak white guy."

"And like just because I'm half black I love fried chicken and watermelon," she had snapped.

With that, she had wrapped her arms around him, looked him straight in the eyes and told him to promise her he'd never, ever again put himself down.

He realized now that Sonja had been the best thing that ever happened to him. While they both never had professed that they loved each other, they certainly had a grand time together. She of a refined, genteel nature who was into reading, classical music and fine dining. He the rough, masculine, anything goes character who was the prototypical country and western music redneck.

They had laid low in their relationship because, alas, Sonja was a married woman. Her much older (and immensely more financially well off) husband was terminally ill. Had been in Hospice for months. Could barely speak and seemed, after the first few weeks of being in a care facility, not even to recognize his wife.

David said just a few of the right kinds of pills placed discreetly in her husband's mouth would make her a free woman, but Sonja always refused.

So Sonja Powers and David Patrick Jackson III had an understanding. They would make each other happy in every way—emotionally, mentally, physically. And she would stay married—as she often reminded David of her wedding vows—"till death do us part."

She would faithfully visit her gravely ill, barely aware husband in the care facility, maintain the image of a caring, devoted wife and keep living in her and her husband's residence. David had accepted all this wholeheartedly—as long as he and Sonja could occasionally rendezvous or escape for a short out-of-town trip.

And so this tacit, mutually beneficial arrangement played out over several months.

Sonja kept trying to convince herself that God didn't want her to be miserable, and so He had placed David Patrick Jackson III in her life. But even if that were true, she had a hard time with it.

David's mantra to her was to just go with the flow because her divine creator realized that she was a woman with certain needs—that couldn't be squelched just because her husband was for all practical purposes already gone.

Tears welling up in her eyes, Sonja would nod knowingly and ask him to hold her tenderly and never let her go. "I know what we're doing is wrong, David," she whispered, all the while rubbing her wedding ring behind David's neck. "Just plain not right. But I can't stand to live without you. Don't ever leave me, please!"

Not that Sonja and David could be together every day or night, but when it did work out that they could connect, what a connection it had been!

They had gone shopping and to movies and dinner and danced together to their hearts content—always doing this at least an hour's drive out of town. Money had been no object, because Sonja had unlimited access to her husband's bank account.

And the really sizzling times had occurred when they could escape overnight to the coast—about four hours' drive away. Oh, the salt air, sand, breeze and ocean! Something about the Carolina coast smacked of romance, fun, excitement, wildnesss. The perfect escape for David Patrick Jackson III and the ostensibly grieving Mrs. Sonja Powers. A beachside getaway where you could get lost. Where you could play, laugh, act crazy, shag till your heart's content, totally let yourself go.

And it had all gone so very well until that day they went scuba diving. So sunny and warm and the ocean so blue and sleepily calm in a cove where they'd decided to dive. Sea birds hung in the air, and near the horizon they could see sailboats and just a hint of thin clouds. The wind caressed and soothed.

Eager to explore, swim and deepen her tan, Sonja had looked fabulous in her two-piece.

And then the unthinkable had happened.

Sonja let out a blood curdling scream. She went under. Arms thrashing and yelling frantically for help, she bobbed back to the surface.

David, who'd just emerged from the water and was standing on the beach, raced back into the ocean.

But when she screamed "Shark!" he stopped cold.

"Shark! Shark! It's killing me!" Sonja wailed.

And that's exactly what the bull shark did.

When they retrieved her mangled body, her legs and arms had suffered severe bites. The ferocious fish, apparently angry that its domain had been disturbed, had chomped down on her torso, pulled her under the water and attacked her face and neck.

The woman who had dreamed of scuba diving—who had told David that she wanted to swim with dolphins and find treasure on the ocean floor—was gone.

And David Patrick Jackson III was never the same. He quit his job—a good job with benefits as an insurance adjuster. He broke off all ties with his family. He turned first to alcohol, then to drugs. He'd gotten a doctor to prescribe opioids for him—to escape, to lose himself in a dark, depressing world where he cared nothing about anyone, let alone himself. And then he'd become addicted to the powerful prescription painkillers—not able to go even a few hours without swallowing one.

Realizing what was happening, his doctor stopped the prescriptions and urged David to commit himself to a mental hospital and go into therapy for clinical depression.

David Patrick Jackson III, wallowing in his dystopian world, adamantly and angrily refused. And so a life of crime—to feed his opioid habit—ensued. He had quickly learned that there was good money to be had by selling opioids on the streets.

His became a miserable, dark existence where the memories of his passionate relationship with Mrs. Sonja Powers quickly faded. Too painful and pointless to recall any of that.

And then, completely out of the blue, came another life-changing event.

After a late night of drinking at a tiki bar on the coast of Carolina, not far from where Sonja had died about a year earlier, he had decided to walk down the beach.

It was summer. A warm wind blew his baseball cap off and David remembered bending down to retrieve it. When he rose, he looked upward. The cloudless night had a million stars and a spectacular pale yellow moon. Waves crashed against the shore. He thought he could hear the heavy breathing of a loggerhead turtle. *She's laying her eggs,* David thought. *But where exactly? Maybe a little ways up that big dune to my left?*

So he had started walking briskly, totally alone, he thought, toward the sound of the turtle.

Except he had not been alone.

He had knelt down to get a better view of the loggerhead when out of nowhere, it seemed, two men clad in black jumped him. How could I have not heard them? David would ask himself later. But then he had realized the beer had dulled his senses.

Both of the attackers, judging from their accents, were Hispanics. One of them, a tall angular, muscular man with a piercing in his lip and a pony tail, had a handgun. His shorter counterpart had a length of rope, the kind suitable for binding a person's legs and arms.

The tall one held the gun barrel to David's right temple and shouted in broken English that if his captive didn't do exactly as they said, he'd die.

So with one of the men holding him hostage with the gun and the other shoving him in the back toward the ocean, the three of them moved closer to the waves.

"What are we doing? Where are we goin'?! Who are you?!" David asked.

But the men in black were in no mood for questions. Far from it.

They kept pushing him toward the sea.

And then one of them said, "Senor, you make big mistake dating the wife of our boss. And not only that, you *kill* his wife. And now you pay!"

"But I didn't kill her. A shark did!"

"But you could have saved her life!" the Mexican pushing him in the back yelled. "You nothin' but a worthless piece of trash!"

The sand was getting wetter and more packed, and the waves were louder.

Only a few more feet to the ocean.

Was the man pushing him in the back armed? David didn't know. What he did know was that one of his accosters had a gun barrel pressed to his temple. He could also discern, from their broken English, that he was about to be hogtied. Their plan, apparently, was to put a bullet in him, tie his hands and feet so that even if he survived the gunshot, he wouldn't be able to move. And then dump him in the ocean.

But he knew one crucial thing that they didn't know. He had a six-inch switchblade knife strapped inside his pants to the lower part of his left leg. Always kept that trusty little sticker with him when he went out drinking or carousing.

Right now the blade, sharp as a razor, was folded in its handle. But push a button and it would spring out quick as lightning.

"Senor, we shoot you first. But we don't try to kill you. We hurt you very bad. Then we drag you out into the ocean and let the fish and the birds eat your carcass. They will eat you slowly and you will suffer very much, just like the woman you lured away from her husband and let die," the man with the handgun yelled.

"Te mueres ahora!" the other one said with a laugh.

Figuring he had nothing to lose, David made his move.

He slapped the gun away from his head, surprised with how fast he moved, and spun quickly around toward the man at his back.

Who by this time was on the ground with his obscenity-spewing friend searching for the weapon in the advancing waves.

The gun hadn't traveled very far. In fact, it was right there at their feet.

Black clad man number one bent down to retrieve it, but it was too late.

Because by that time, David had gotten his switchblade out, pressed the button and started slashing.

And not only slashing and stabbing, but doing it with a vengeance. So quickly and so deeply did he cut that the man's head was practically removed from his body.

And black-clad man number two?

He begged for mercy and began backing away. Swore he would never tell anyone what had happened. Held his hands up in supplication. Grovelled.

"Vamos!" David demanded, not even sure of what that word meant.

Black-clad man two ran for his life, while David just stood there in the blood and sand and carnage—sure that his little unfortunate happening was over, for good.

But no way, as it turned out, was that the last of it.

For the man that got away would tell his boss—David's girlfriend's husband—what had happened, and the husband, who had made something of a miraculous recovery from a coma, would contact the police. *Or was it that Sonja had been lying about her husband's condition all along?*

An investigation would turn into a he said/she said proposition, with David left trying to explain why he had decapitated a law-abiding, upstanding brown citizen who just had happened to be on the beach that night.

The bit about the Mexican holding a gun to David's temple and he and his accomplice pushing him toward the ocean? The police and court didn't buy it. Nor were the authorities won over by David's adamant contention that he'd acted in self defense. And, as it turned out, the tall guy had a permit to legally carry the gun with him wherever he went. And who wouldn't want to have a gun with them while going for a stroll late at night on a beach?

The result: David Patrick Jackson III was found guilty of one count of second-degree murder and sentenced to 12 years in state prison in West Tabor City, N.C.

And now here he was, a serial killer on the prowl for opioids in mountainous East Tennessee. Strangling old, helpless women who lived in a part of the country once inhabited by the legendary Davy Crockett and Daniel Boone.

Feeding his habit. Killing. Striking fast and deadly and slithering away stealthily to this old weather-beaten trailer hidden among the woods.

Then plotting his next move and bracing himself against the cold, biting wind and snow that he could smell in the air. The natural elements would only worsen, for sure, and when they did, David Patrick Jackson III wanted to be far away from East Tennessee. Not a smart move, he figured, to tempt fate—whether that be someone from the law knocking on his trailer door or a vicious winter storm blowing right through the thin walls of his flimsy shelter.

The thought of snowflakes swirling through his sorry excuse for a door sent shivers up his spine. Well, not quite as sorry as that quilt he'd had hanging at the entrance to keep the chill out. He had managed a few weeks ago to fashion a piece of plywood into a makeshift door. Because he didn't want to freeze to death. No way.

Better for this old bird to spread his wings and fly outta' here.

Chapter 14
Heat on the Press

In the bustling newsroom of the *News-Journal*, everyone breathed a sigh of relief. It was early Wednesday afternoon and they had just put the next day's edition to bed.

"Congrats, folks!" a tired but satisfied editor Dudley Lowery said to his staff. "Another rough draft of history is in the hopper."

Outside the wide one-story building of the *News-Journal*, snow had begun to fall. The temperature had plunged to around 30 degrees. The air was cold but invigorating. Folks wondered if the snow signaled the beginning of a cold snap. Or was this a sign that the inevitable winter would be long and bitter? Already, a big snowstorm had begun wreaking havoc a few hundred miles away in the Northeast. Folks in Summer's Rest were tracking that paralyzing storm the last couple of days on the national news.

Lowery didn't have much time to ponder such, although he did make it a point, after commending his staff, to gaze out his office window at his bird-feeders. What he saw reminded him that there was something in this life much more glorious than a newspaper. Wide-eyed, he took in the icy flakes dropping from the sky, amid quite an array of bird life. The editor had been a birder since his college days. While others of his generation immersed themselves in such spectator sports as basketball and football, he preferred the quiet magic of nature. Birds, especially, had been his passion.

And here, within a few arm lengths of his office window, they were in all their splendor at his two hanging birdfeeders. Robins, bluejays, cardinals and finches were his feathered guests today.

Suddenly the spell was broken.

A hulking, red-faced man who appeared to be a farmer had burst into the newsroom. Lowery knew right off that the man hadn't come here to thank him for a job well done. Instead, the malcontent obviously had a fish to fry. The editor braced himself for the worst.

Meanwhile, publisher Jake Cravens had overheard the commotion and stuck his head out his office door. But when he saw the complainant he ducked back inside. *Trouble with a capital T*, Cravens thought. *I can't think of that SOB's name but I've heard he's quare.*

"Mister editor man! I'd like a word with you right now!"

Swallowing hard, Lowery invited him inside and asked him to take a seat.

"I ain't a feelin' like sittin' down!" he said pointedly. "I been readin' this danged newspaper for pert near 20 years, and I now I'm wantin' you to not publish somethin' that's personal and private."

"And what would that be, sir?" Lowery asked.

The red-faced man, in dirty overalls and high top rubber boots, flicked his John Deere cap a bit farther back on his head.

Then, pointing his finger at the nervous editor, he continued: "What I'm sayin' is this: I done bought a piece'a property up on Reece Ridge and it ain't nobidy's business. And I ain't wantin' nobidy to know what I paid fer it!"

The editor responded calmly: "Sir, if that transaction was recorded at the Taylor County courthouse, it'll appear in the *News-Journal*. That's because we don't make any exceptions when it comes to publishing the public record. All the land transfers—the names of the buyer and seller, the price paid for the property and the location and acreage—all of this appears in our newspaper."

"I'm warnin' you, young man!" the man declared angrily. "If one word of my personal bizness gets printed in this damned rag, you'll regret it!"

Lowery tried to stay calm, explaining to the man again that when it came to publishing the public record, the *News-Journal* made no exceptions for anyone.

But the snarling, cursing farmer was having none of that. He tightened his jaws and shook his right fist at the editor.

"I done spoke my piece! You ain't even from Taylor County! You need to get your ass outta this town!"

He stomped out of the office like a snorting bull—the rest of the newsroom staff doing their best to act as if nothing had just happened.

After Lowery was sure that the man was no longer in the building, he quickly called a staff meeting.

"Ladies and gentlemen," he announced, "if we don't print but one property transfer in next week's edition of the Public Record, I want us to be doubly certain that it's that man's land transaction."

A couple of reporters broke into a mild applause as publisher Jake Cravens joined the meeting.

Straightening his suit jacket and holding a Cuban cigar in his right hand, the publisher announced: "My granddaddy started this paper and if there's one thing he stood for in his long, storied life, it was freedom of the press.

"And that means nobody orders us what to print or what not to print—ever!" Cravens thundered. "And the more they don't want something published, the more we'll run it!"

More soft, polite applause from the newsroom as Cravens, happy with himself, began walking back to his office. But he stopped when a worried-looking front desk clerk motioned that she needed desperately to speak with him.

"What is it, Miss Bonnie?"

"Sir, it's that delegation of concerned citizens again. They're demanding that you meet with them." She spoke sheepishly, almost apologetically.

"What're they wantin' this time?" Cravens puffed on his cigar. "Don't they know the sheriff's doin' everything in his power to catch that serial killer? What we're runnin' here is a newspaper, not a business that tries to keep everybody happy. We just report the news. We don't make it."

"They're sayin', sir, that you're in cahoots with the sheriff and you won't print anything negative about him," the small framed woman said meekly. "They're wantin' fairness in journalism."

"Tell 'em to write a letter to the editor!" Cravens snapped. "No bunch of busy bodies tells me how to run my newspaper."

Ignoring the desk clerk's entreaties to be patient while she summoned her boss, a leader of the Concerned Citizens barged into the newsroom: "Mr. Cravens, we'd like to speak with you! And we're not leavin' this newspaper till you hear us out!"

The publisher noticed that behind the adamant spokeswoman were about a dozen people—and they seemed to be getting antsier and more demanding by the second. He reluctantly motioned for them to come inside his office. Then he instructed Bonnie to bring him some more chairs so as to make the visitors more comfortable.

Their leader looked to be about a hundred pounds overweight. She declined to take a seat—instead hiking up her baggy jeans by the belt loops, shifting her body slightly and pulling her sweater down over her waist so as to hide the top of her butt crack.

"Now, Mr. Cravens, I've lived in Summer's Rest for 20 years and I know the real deal about your newspaper. We didn't come here to listen to you spew a bunch of BS about freedom of the press and how you treat everybidy the same."

The publisher flinched but kept quiet for a few seconds. Then he erupted. "I'm not going to sit here and listen to you insult my newspaper, ladies and gentlemen!" he barked. "Because if that's what you're plannin' to do—run my newspaper down—you can get your fannies outta here right now!"

When the leader of the group bared her teeth and made a motion as if she were about to charge headfirst into the chief executive of the local press, she was restrained by another woman in the group. She was a redhead in stylishly frayed skinny jeans and knee-high brown boots. Her short zippered jacket—not something that would keep you warm on such a cold day outside, bore the words (in gold cursive letters) LOVE, JOY & CHEER.

At least maybe somebody I can reason with, the publisher thought.

But woman number two's looks were deceiving. She was just as much a bulldog on the prowl as the group leader. When she was confident that she had the publisher's full attention—and that the leader would defer to her—she spoke. "We're not here to burn this place down. All we want is a fair shake. We want you to report ALL the news, not just some of it."

Jake Cravens just stared at her and said nothing for a few seconds. His eyes were drawn to the hint of pink underwear showing in the holes just below her pockets. Meanwhile, others in the group of malcontents jostled about and mumbled their discontent.

Then he spoke: "Just spit it out. What specifically is it that you want from the *News-Journal*?"

Woman number one shouted: "We don't want your newspaper to knuckle under to the sheriff's office! We're wantin' you to print the truth, the whole truth and nothin' but the truth, so help you God!"

Cravens bolted up from his chair: "This ain't a damned courtroom! So just cut out all that legal talk. Y'all can just get your meddlin' butts out of my office!"

A distinguished looking silver-haired man, clearing his throat, interjected: "Not until you print a story about the sexual harassment charge against Sheriff Coffmann. And not until you give us your word of honor that you'll run a front page piece—every day—about what the police are doing to catch that serial killer."

"What sexual harassment charge?" Cravens asked incredulously.

Woman number one said: "Well, the lawsuit against Sheriff Coffmann ain't exactly been filed yet, but we have it on good authority that'll happen any day now. Young lady swears that when she was 16—and Coffmann was 30—he done tried to take some liberties with her. Asked her to take her blouse off while he dropped his britches. She got real spooked and ran to her momma."

Cravens rubbed his brow, straightened his tie and took a deep breath. He had been caught off guard by what he intuited was a group of petulant busybodies. And he had been ambushed in the worst way—something he never liked.

The publisher asked, "So what does Sheriff Coffmann say about all this?"

"Of course, he's living in that DEE-NI-EL river," said woman number one, hitching up her jeans again.

Cravens snickered. "I'll tell you what, folks, if and when such a bogus lawsuit is filed, we will report on it chapter and verse, and we'll include our good sheriff's side of the story. But not until a complaint is filed at the courthouse. Y'all clear about that?"

The silver-haired gentleman, as stoic as ever, didn't take his eyes off the publisher. "So that brings us, Mr. Cravens, to the matter of how your newspaper plans to keep the pressure on the authorities with catching this serial killer. Will you promise you'll print a front page update every day on what the police are doing on this case? Maybe run a picture of one'a them hour glasses that shows how long it's been since the first murder, the second murder and the third murder?"

"Nobody orders me how to run my newspaper! We're professionals here! We do the right thing! We print the truth each and every day!"

The group listened as the publisher continued pontificating fervently on how the *News-Journal* was the "soul of this community" and couldn't be pushed around by anyone.

Then a diminutive, frail woman in her eighties hobbled with her cane to the front of the group and spoke up softly.

Cravens hadn't noticed her before, but now he instantly recognized Mrs. Mabel Ada Hopkins. Her grandfather had founded the First National Bank of Summer's Rest. Her father had been the president and now had passed the baton of bank leadership to her—where she served as the bank's CEO and chair of the board of directors.

A hush came over the room as Mrs. Hopkins said: "You can save your breath on all that highfalutin mumbo-jumbo stuff about truth and freedom of the press, Mr. Cravens. Because if you don't do as we ask about keeping that stuff about this serial killer on your front page, I promise you your newspaper will lose its most lucrative advertising contract—$200,000 a year with the First National Bank.

"And I personally know just about every business owner in Summer's Rest. I can pick up the phone easy as pie and they'll do as I say. My bank'll start its own newspaper."

Cravens smiled meekly. "Of course, Mrs. Hopkins. I hadn't seen you back there. My paper'll be more than glad to do as you say."

Woman number one piped up smugly: "That's because you're free to print whatever she wants you to print. And don't you forget it, you pompous SOB!"

The man with the silver hair put his two cents in, saying, "It's a curious thing this idea we call freedom of the press."

Cravens was speechless but relieved. He summoned his desk clerk to bring everyone in the group a hot cup of coffee or hot chocolate (their choice, he announced) and a fresh doughnut.

"It's been my pleasure and honor speaking with y'all today," he said. "Now y'all just make yourselves at home. Would any of you like a complimentary one-year subscription to the best newspaper in Summer's Rest and Taylor County?"

Woman number one grunted to woman number two, "It's our ONLY local paper."

Chapter 15
Self-Reflecting

It took only a few minutes for Jake Cravens to call his close friend High Sheriff Ethan Coffmann about the delegation of Concerned Citizens who'd descended on the *News-Journal.*

"It's bad, my friend," Cravens told him. "They're accusing you of doing something sexual with a teenage girl way back years ago. Refused to divulge her name. I personally think it's horse manure but I'm just letting you know."

What else can they hit me with? Coffmann wondered. He also couldn't imagine what female would concoct such a thing against him. Yes, he'd been a little crazy in his early days or even in the early part of his marriage to Laura, but he'd never strayed. And never, ever would have come on to a teenager.

But then again, this was the climate we found ourselves in today, the sheriff reminded himself. He was in a position of power and respect, at least until recently, but some devious person could easily bring him down.

Ready to do him in. Destroy his reputation, humiliate his family and take away everything he'd ever worked for.

"So are you going to print that trash?" Coffmann asked the publisher. "Because if you do, I'm ruined."

Cravens assured him that nothing about the accusation would appear in the paper unless.

"Unless what?" the sheriff asked pointedly. He despised it when Cravens took that sanctimonious, know-it-all tone.

"Unless she actually files a lawsuit, Ethan. And then it becomes part of the public record. Anyone can simply sashay over to the courthouse and read a copy of it. Not a thing we can do to keep it on the downlow.

"Sorry, Ethan."

The embattled sheriff had heard all this malarkey about the public record before. He was convinced that it was simply another way for Cravens to sell more newspapers.

'I'll tell you what, Jake. Go ahead and print that garbage and it'll be a cold day in hell before you get another speck of news from my office. You can just warn your bloodsucking reporters to stay away from here!"

"Now, Ethan, calm down. I'd say they're bluffing. I'll bet no such accusation will ever see the light of day. And even if it does, remember we'll print your side of the story."

Big fat consolation, the sheriff thought bitterly. But he held his tongue.

After a few awkward seconds, the sheriff asked, "Any other good news you've got for me?"

The publisher told him about how the group had demanded that his newspaper run a front page article every day about the status of the murder investigation.

"They're sayin' everybody is real scared. The public's itchin' for answers. They want to know what you're doing to catch this serial killer. And they're saying it's just a matter of time before he strikes again."

The sheriff wasn't happy but he'd also expected as much. "And so your damned newspaper is putting my office on notice that the sheriff's office better catch this guy soon or else…"

The publisher explained to him how Mrs. Mabel Ada Hopkins had given him an ultimatum.

"So you sold out, didn't you? You and your newspaper can spout all this freedom of the press and high and mighty truth and fairness stuff, but when it gets right down to it, you're for sale by the highest bidder? You're no better than the corner produce stand or the dirty book store. Ain't that what it amounts to?"

The publisher couldn't take any more. His blood pressure rising, he slammed the receiver down and lit another cigar. Then he barked an order to his editor to get a graphic artist involved in the daily update of the murders.

"I want art and it's got to be compelling—something along the lines of a chart or hourglass showing what law enforcement is doing to catch this serial killer! And I want a story to accompany it every day. Package all this in some sort of box with a gripping red 80-point headline so that it gets everybody's attention on the front page. Do I make myself clear?"

Editor Lowery said he'd make sure all that was done, and then he made the mistake of asking why?

"Because, first of all, I said so! And second, if we don't do this, we won't have a newspaper!" Cravens screamed.

Meanwhile, back at the sheriff's office, Ethan Coffmann had told his deputies that he'd be gone for a few hours while he patrolled the county. What he didn't tell them was that he needed sanctuary and that where he found it was in his Crown Vic police cruiser—where no one could threaten him or ruin his day.

The police car was High Sheriff Ethan Coffmann's comfort zone. His escape hatch. His therapy. A place where he could drive and meditate and self-reflect. As he headed toward the outskirts of town, the sheriff began asking himself what it was, if anything, he could do, to keep his enemies at bay. *But then again, what does it really matter what anyone thinks about me?*

He harkened back to a sermon at church that he and Laura had heard last Sunday. He couldn't remember the exact words, but the gist of it, from Proverbs, was this: We are not defined by what we do or not do or by our accomplishments or failures. Instead, what really matters—what's significant in this short life we have this side of eternity—is who we truly are.

The minister that day had urged his listeners to consider these questions: What's at our core? What do we value most in life? Who do we love? Who are we, really? The answers to those deep questions are what actually defines us—not what others think about us or our reputation in the community.

Religion usually went in one ear and out the other for lukewarm believer Ethan Coffmann, but today, for whatever reason, that Sunday sermon resonated.

It made perfect sense not to get overly caught up in the ups and downs of this world, the sheriff told himself. But then again, he was also aware that we're all human. We all care, whether we admit it or not, about what others think about us. *I've worked my butt off my whole life to build and protect my reputation, to keep my marriage strong and to uphold the law and keep people safe, but now all that's hanging by a thin thread.*

To help take his mind off himself, he pulled slowly into Heaven's Valley Cemetery. He had noticed a funeral procession headed that way a few minutes earlier, and sure enough, there on a steep grassy hill of the cemetery was a small gathering of people. Bundled up against the biting cold, they had huddled together under a green funeral awning. Next to the group of mourners was an open grave. A flag-draped pine casket was about to be lowered. Because it was a veteran being laid to rest, Sheriff Coffmann decided to stop his car.

He walked slowly to the graveside.

One of the mourners urged him to join them. No politics here. No resentment or fear or threats. Just a group of family and friends saying farewell to their loved one. United and somber in death.

High Sheriff Ethan Coffmann removed his hat, placed it on his heart, saluted the old soldier he had never personally known and listened to the graveside eulogy. A man, who appeared to be in his late 60s—possibly the deceased's son, Coffmann thought—wept next to the coffin as a minister tried to say a few words of comfort and encouragement.

"Our dearly beloved Nathaniel Jenkins, age 99, led a good, fulfilling life as a member of the Greatest Generation," the young clergyman said. "That's what we can say of those—such as Nathaniel—who endured the tribulations of the Great Depression and then went on to selflessly serve our country in World War II."

The Jenkins name was still visible in faded letters on the side of a retail building in the small downtown, but Ethan assumed the younger generation had moved away, as he didn't personally recognize any of them.

"And today, as we say goodbye to Mr. Jenkins, we can truly say, with all our hearts that he loved his family, his church, his community and his country. What better or more exalted life could a man have led?

"Mr. Jenkins was a veteran of the U.S. Navy and served as an elder in his church. He always put his faith and family foremost in his life."

They were words that spoke to Sheriff Coffmann's heart. *With all this mess going on, have I put my family first in my life? What'll they say about me when I'm gone?*

The sheriff felt a gentle mountain breeze. He and the rest of the little group were standing there under a cloudy sky that threatened rain—and maybe even snow. But the wet stuff held off as the plain pine coffin was lowered into the grave at the pastoral cemetery and a military honors color guard fired three shots.

A crisply dressed U.S. Marine Corps private reverently folded an American flag and presented it to the man, still weeping, next to where the coffin had been lowered. "This is on behalf of the president of the United States," the Marine said.

The graveside service—simple but profound—ended with a solemn prayer—thanking the Lord for Nathaniel Jenkins' life and requesting comfort for his grieving family and friends.

Glad that he had been there to be with a fellow veteran who had obviously made a difference in so many people's lives, the sheriff put his hat back on, waved slightly to the family and walked alone back to his police cruiser. No sooner had he pulled away than his radio blared out: "Taylor County one, Taylor County one, are you there?"

"Roger," the sheriff answered. *Not another killing, please.*

"Please return to home base immediately, sir. The publisher of the *News-Journal* is in your office with another fella. Don't know what they want but they say it's urgent."

"Ten-four and roger that. Returning now," said the sheriff, irritated that his escape from the office had been so brief. *Now what in God's name could Jake Cravens be up to now?*

When he arrived at his office about a half hour later, Cravens was there pacing the floor with Donald Mink, his graphic artist. The diminutive Donald—his last name rhymes with pink, he always told everyone—sat nonchalantly in an oak chair in front of Coffmann's desk.

The sheriff had never personally met Donald but he'd seen his car, a 1981 blue VW Beetle, around town. On the rear window of the vehicle were two stickers. One screamed "BACK OFF! GAY ON BOARD!" The other said "QUEERDO." A beaded necklace hung from the front windshield mirror. A yellow girlie-looking flower stuck out next to the steering wheel.

To say that Donald's car called attention to itself would be an understatement. Everywhere he went, people stared. And if they happened to be near Donald as he opened the car door, there were plenty of whispers—most of them about his sexual orientation.

"Good afternoon, Ethan," the publisher said as the sheriff walked right by him, without so much as a handshake, and took his seat behind his desk.

When the sheriff nodded, the publisher, a twinkle in his eyes, introduced his guest. "Donald here is the best danged graphic artist in these parts. He's a genius with cartoons, graphs, charts and sketches. We are extremely honored to have him at the *News-Journal*."

Coffmann said nothing. Instead he just kept his seat and sized up the young man Cravens had brought with him. He already knew about Donald's car, but this was the first time he'd met the man himself. And when you saw him, you didn't soon forget him.

With piercings in his nose and bottom lip and a Mohawk haircut, Donald stood out in a crowd. He had a pale wan face, a skinny neck, light pink hair and effeminate features, including soft, small hands with polished nails and brightly rouged, rosy cheeks. Had he been a woman, he would have been a passably cute one.

Cravens noticed that the sheriff wasn't exactly starstruck by his graphic artist. Instead, it was more like Coffmann couldn't believe such a person was actually gainfully employed in Summer's Rest.

"He's the very best at what he does, Ethan," Cravens continued, trying to snap the sheriff out of his ruminations. "And that's why I've brought him here with me today."

The sheriff once again said nothing. He just sat there stoically, with his elbows on his desk.

"What I mean, Ethan, is that Donald here can sketch a likeness of anyone—without ever having seen them. All you do is describe that person to him and he can draw them. And not just draw them, but make 'em seem like they posed for him."

The sheriff was intrigued but mystified. Intrigued that this little gay blade named Donald could be so good at sketching. And mystified as to why the publisher was telling him all this.

"Just think of Donald here as a forensic sketch artist. He's ready and willin' to help your department find our serial killer."

"But we don't have any witnesses!" the astounded sheriff replied. "So there's nobody could tell him what the killer looks like. You know that and I know that."

The publisher was unfazed. He reminded the sheriff that they had that composite profile description of the suspect. And what would be the harm in letting Donald create a sketch from it?

The sheriff objected: "But he's not seen the killer! Nobody's seen him except the victims and they're all three dead! He's got no damned description to work with."

"He's got that composite profile description that we've already published in our newspaper and will continue to publish," Cravens said. "Let's see what he comes up with."

The sheriff was still unconvinced, but a side of him thought it wasn't the most far out idea he'd ever heard. *Let the little pointy-eared queer have at it,* he mused. After all, police sketch artists had played a pivotal role in helping catch the Unabomber Ted Kaczynski and Tim McVeigh, the Oklahoma City Federal Building bomber.

On the other hand, a forensic sketch artist could also do damage. The sheriff remembered reading about a rape suspect who had been falsely accused and convicted and imprisoned, after he'd been fingered in a police lineup based on a sketch. In hindsight, the witness—the rape victim—had simply been too traumatized to accurately describe the man who had attacked her. So the sketch drawn by the police artist had been faulty.

To the skeptical sheriff's mind, creating an image of a suspect, as described by a witness, was part science and part art, and was tricky at best. Because how reliable is a witness' memory when it comes to trying to convey to a sketch artist such things as the suspect's lips, nose, eyes, eyebrows, hair and ears?

So yes, police sketch artists were potentially valuable for law enforcement, but what they did was controversial and dicey. And what of an artist, no matter how talented, creating a sketch without a witness?

The publisher listened to all this but pressed his case. "Let's give my man Donald here a chance. Let him draw our suspect—or at least what he thinks our man might look like. And we'll print it on the front page of the *News-Journal*."

"I still don't like it, and besides, how do I really know that Donald is as good as you say he is?"

"Well, suit yourself, Ethan. Give him a tryout. Describe to him somebody you know but that he's never seen. Let him put together a sketch of that person. See what he comes up with."

Still not convinced, the sheriff said, "This isn't America's Most Wanted. We're not playing games here. And we're not into entertainment. I'm a busy man, Jake!"

"Give him a tryout," the publisher implored. "Judge for yourself."

The exasperated sheriff punched a button on his phone receiver. "Mattie, please come in here right now."

When the young woman, one of his combination desk clerks and dispatchers, entered the office, he asked her to have a seat. Then the sheriff explained to her that Donald would be asking her a few questions about someone in her family—that Donald had never met—and creating a sketch of the person from her answers.

Mattie, reveling in the spotlight, batted her eyes, straightened her skirt, crossed her legs and threw her shoulders back. She said she'd be glad to help any way she could. And after Donald assured her that he'd never laid eyes on her husband, she began describing him.

He asked for a glass of water, pulled up a chair directly in front of her and pulled out his sketch pad. His pointed questions came quickly, and throughout the interview, he sketched lightly, and seemingly effortlessly, with his artist's pencil.

"Is your husband white? African-American? Asian? Mexican?

"How old is he?

"What's his hair like? Long? Short? Sideburns? Mustache? Beard?

"What's his hairline like? Does he have a widow's peak?

"How would you describe his face? Long? Wide? Round? About average or normal in shape? Any moles or freckles?

"What about his nose? Is it fat? Skinny? Thin?

"Describe his eyes. Do they seem close together? Far apart? About average in distance apart from each other?

"What about his eyebrows? Thin? Bushy? Thick?

"How about his mouth and lips? Anything distinctive about them?"

And so it went for about an hour.

Jake Cravens paced. He puffed on his cigar and kept glancing at his watch. To help pass the time, he formed a picture in his mind of what Mattie might have looked like in high school. Bet she was quite the peach, he thought.

Trying to maintain an aura of politeness, Ethan Coffmann kept checking his smartphone. He noticed on Yahoo News that another highly respected public official had resigned; one of his young female aides had alleged sexual harassment.

Mattie, chatterbox that she was in daily life, seemed to love the attention.

Donald drew. Every so often he'd close his eyes and pause, as if waiting for inspiration. Then he'd open them and erase a few lines. And resume drawing.

Finally, after 60 minutes, Donald announced that he was finished. He handed his portrait interview-based sketch—of the person he'd never personally seen—to his interviewee, Mattie.

"Oh my gosh!" she gasped. "That's a spitting image of my husband Rick!"

Sheriff Coffmann asked her if she had a picture of Rick in her purse or on her phone.

Within moments, she showed them one. And, yes, the sheriff and the publisher could see that the resemblance was uncanny.

Little gay Donald with the piercings and the QUEERDO sticker on his car's rear window had almost perfectly captured a likeness of a man he'd never seen in person.

Nevertheless, Ethan Coffmann was still unconvinced. “Like I said before, we don’t have a witness who your sketcher can interview. It’d be a shot in the dark at best.”

Cravens looked his old friend straight in the eye and said: “It’s the only shot we have. Let him do the drawing from that composite profile and let me publish it.”

“I’ll take it under advisement” was the best the publisher could get out of him.

Chapter 16
Chasing the Wind

The sheriff didn't stay undecided about Donald very long. For the next day, after several persistent requests from a salivating-for-a-scoop Jake Cravens, he caved.

"Yes, let your man Donald have at it," Coffmann had finally said. "And no, don't come whining to me when we're all the laughingstock of the town. Whoever heard of a sketch artist doing his thing without talking to a witness who had seen the criminal? Personally, I think we're just chasing the wind."

Coffmann had only reluctantly let the publisher convince him. He remembered, for example, the woman who'd sat down with a police forensic artist and gave her description of the Unabomber. She'd seen the suspect for all of about three seconds at a post office. But still it had been a glimpse—enough for the artist to come up with something that had helped the police. With this serial killer case, the authorities had no living witness. What they did have was conjecture, theory, educated guesses at best.

True, the FBI forensics people had created a composite profile of who they were looking for: white male, in his late 20s or early 30s, muscular build with bulging biceps, a barrel chest, broad shoulders and a thick tree-trunk like neck, facial hair—likely a beard and maybe an unkempt mustache—long hair, over six feet tall and weighing more than 200 pounds, size 14 shoe, a loner with big rough hands who kept to himself, worked in construction or performed manual labor, probably had been previously convicted of a violent crime and served time in prison.

So the sheriff had a profile but it was all conjecture. He had no visual. No likeness. Nothing, essentially, other than an idea, albeit one promulgated by the best forensic minds in the business—of what the suspect might look like and his approximate age, height, weight and build.

On the other hand, he'd been told that the main objective of a sketch was not for it to be a perfect match of the person police were seeking. The point was to produce a resemblance, however crude, so that the public might think of someone they'd seen who possibly could be that suspect. Some police sketch artists had summed up what they did as eliminating the indisputably innocent and pointing the finger at those who might be guilty.

But that bothered the sheriff. What if some bozo saw the sketch in the newspaper and thought of it as a dead ringer for his next door neighbor? So he calls the police and says Johnny living right beside him looks like the killer. Police check it out and it's a dead end. Johnny, who has an airtight alibi, is humiliated, embarrassed and angry. He calls a lawyer.

Another scenario: The real killer sees the sketch and profile description. He does one of two things. One, he laughs his ass off because the police are so far off base that he figures they won't catch him in a million years, and he continues his rampage of killing. Two, he sees a distinct resemblance, gets nervous and changes, as much as he can, what he looks like. Plus, he leaves the area.

Another thing concerned the sheriff. He was 99 percent certain that the suspect had been convicted of a serious crime. But if that were the case, why wasn't there a match of his DNA in the National DNA Database? The killer had left all sorts of genetic material on his victims—including follicles of his hair and even his blood. Each one of the old women had tried to resist him—had struggled mightily, the sheriff figured—to fight him off. Had punched and flailed about and scratched him. The evidence-minded suspect had removed their night clothes, bedsheets, pillow cases and blankets and taken those with him.

What he hadn't removed was his own blood—from beneath their fingernails—and traces of his semen in or around their vaginas. He might have worn a condom because he'd left only microscopic traces. But what was that old saying? You don't need a gallon of sea water to know that it's salty. Even a trace of bodily fluid on a victim could clinch a case.

But when the TBI and FBI had tried to match the killer's DNA with DNA samples in the National Database, they had come up with nothing. That hadn't convinced Coffmann that his suspect didn't have a criminal record. Because there was always a chance of a glitch in the system. The possibility of a human error—committed by a lab technician or whoever—so that the criminal's DNA had not been documented.

There had been that recent case with the killer who had massacred 26 people at a church in rural Texas. The sheriff recalled reading how years earlier the mentally ill shooter had been jailed and dishonorably discharged from the U.S. Air Force for beating his wife and children.

The murderer assassinated his victims at that Baptist church on a Sunday morning with an assault rifle. Two handguns and hundreds of rounds of ammunition had also been found in his vehicle. The Texas church serial killer never should have been permitted to buy a weapon, but he had easily and legally done so. Because the Air Force had been the glitch in the system. The military had failed, as required by law, to submit the shooter's criminal record to the FBI so that it could be entered into the National Criminal Information Center database.

Sheriff Coffmann was sure this fatal flaw stemmed from a human error—probably committed by a low-ranking airman on a computer somewhere on an Air Force Base in the middle of nowhere. It reminded the sheriff of that bumper sticker he'd seen the other day on Main Street: DEFECATION EVENTUATES. He figured it must have been a visitor with more education than the average citizen.

A few blocks away at his cluttered desk with a flower, nail polish and piles of papers in a corner cubicle of the newsroom at the *News-Journal*, Donald Mink took out his sketch pad and pencil and went to work. But this time he wasn't creating a pie chart of the city's sewer and water system revenues. Nor was he sketching what the new middle school would look like.

Earbuds in his miniature Dr. Spock-like ears and a Diet Coke by his side, the newspaper's graphics artist began sketching, ever so lightly on his easel-mounted pad, a likeness of the criminal suspect that the authorities wanted so desperately to catch. That he had little to go on was an understatement, and some in the newsroom snickered when they heard of his task.

Jasmine Stout, an ad rep, said, "Think he could draw a picture of my granny if I told 'em how much she weighs?"

Rebecca Dunn, circulation assistant, thought that their boss had lost it. "Qeerdo's got it made," she said. "He can draw a picture of anybody he wants and the police'll swallow it hook, line and sinker. We might as well have Barney for our sheriff. Meanwhile, that killer'll strike again—sure as the sun comes up tomorrow."

But Donald paid them no mind. For one thing, with his earbuds piping in rap music from his iPhone, he couldn't hear them. For another, he was in a zone. He had the written profile to help guide him, but Donald also had something else: his intuition and imagination; his gut feelings of what he thought the murderer looked like. Evil had a face of its own. You could picture it in your mind—and even there—it terrified, haunted, attacked.

Donald knew evil—maybe not evil to this degree of darkness, but he knew it. Knew how it felt to be taunted, beat up, bullied, isolated, rejected. How his peers had teased him for his interests in flowers, music, theatre and dancing—instead of baseball, basketball and football.

How a vulnerable, physically weak person, such as himself, had been the target of so many vile, mean, closed-minded people. How, as a teenager, it felt to be so down and depressed that you wanted to commit suicide by jumping off the Rayford Town Bridge—the highest bridge in Taylor County—into the cold blue waters below.

So he sketched and erased and sketched and erased and sketched while he chased three ice-cold Diet Cokes and occasionally sniffed the potted gardenia, his favorite flower which decorated his desk. For three hours.

What he came up with was more a shadowy rendition than a picture of a man's face. He had sketched a large, hulking man whose face appeared to be fuzzy and darkened. The clearest, most prominent features in his portrait were the man's neck (thick as a stovepipe), massive shoulders, arms and hands, and his big clunky shoes. It was rough, yes, but it was at least something.

And something, as far as the publisher of the *News-Journal* was concerned, beat nothing.

Editor Dudley Lowery objected. "Boss, he doesn't have a face. He could be the headless horseman. Who the hell are people supposed to be looking for?"

Cravens shot back: "For somebody big and mean and rough and who has a neck like a tree trunk and big feet! It could be Big Foot for all I care! Don't sweat the details, Mr. Lowery. Now do your job and get Donald's sketch on the front page—in a box with a big headline and juicy story. And increase the press run by 2,000. I have a feelin' we're gonna' sell every paper this side of Johnsonville."

"Shouldn't we first consult with Sheriff Coffmann?"

During that heated exchange, the publisher's secretary motioned for him that he had an urgent phone call from the sheriff's office.

"Hold that thought, young man. But instruct the press room to be ready to run when we give 'em the green light," said Cravens, returning to his private office.

Cupping the phone to his left ear, the publisher muttered, "Ethan, this better be good. Donald's just put the finishing touches on his composite sketch and it ain't half bad. We're ready to roll. Every minute we lollygag is time and a half for those guys on the press."

Sheriff Coffmann said nothing for a few seconds, relishing the thought that Jake Cravens might have to fork out more money than he'd planned for.

"Sheriff, you hearin' me?! You still there?"

"Your little gay Donald can make an even better, more revealing sketch, my friend. I just got off the phone with the Tennessee Bureau of Investigation, and they relayed the highlights of an urgent message from the FBI forensics people."

"You're talking in circles, Ethan. What's this got to do with Donald's sketch?"

The sheriff paused to let the publisher cool off. Plus, he was liking all this. Fine with him that his old friend was getting more ruffled by the second.

“Ethan, are you there, dammit?! I’ve got a paper to put out. Now just spit out whatever it is that’s so earthshaking.”

The sheriff finally spoke: “There’s a new forensic technique. It’s called DNA phenotyping. It’s not perfect, but a person’s DNA can tell us a lot about what that person looks like.

“And guess what? We’ve got plenty of the killer’s DNA.”

A skeptical Jake Cravens contemplated for a few seconds before he spoke. He had watched a lot of “CSI Miami” and never had heard anything about what the sheriff was referring to. “Spell that for me, Sheriff.”

“It’s called phenotyping—pronounced fino-typing. But you spell it: p-h-e-n-o-t-y-p-i-n-g.”

“And how’re they saying it works?”

The sheriff explained, as best he could, what the forensics expert at the TBI had shared with him. A person’s DNA contains genetic markers, and if you know how to interpret those markers, you can come up with a rough idea of what the person’s face looks like. There’s a gene responsible for lip size. Are the lips luscious? Thin? Thick? Another gene determines the shape and curvature of the nose. Other genes are predictive of a person’s facial shape, eye, hair and skin color. There are even genes that can tell you whether a person has freckles.

“So why the hell haven’t I ever heard about this, Sheriff?” said the newspaper publisher, still not entirely convinced but borderline excited.

“Maybe because the technology is so much still in its infancy and they have a long way to make it more revealing.”

“So you’re actually saying, Ethan, that your suspect’s DNA can give us a good clue as to what he looks like?”

“I’m saying that the TBI man told me that they can link DNA genetic markers with a suspect’s physical characteristics.

“But again, keep in mind,” the sheriff cautioned, “that this science is not yet perfect. It needs refining and more study.”

Jake Cravens almost peed in his brand new trousers. “Hell fire! What do we care about more study or some such gobbledygook nonsense? Something’s better than nothing! Tell me what our suspect looks like!”

The sheriff said he'd have one of his deputies hand deliver the killer's DNA phenotype-based physical description to the publisher himself.

"Tell Donald he ain't done yet!" he thundered upon reentering his newsroom, "and tell those ink-stained wretches in the pressroom to hold their horses. "We all just might be gettin' the best Christmas present ever!"

Playing to the moment, Sheriff Coffmann dispatched Deputy Tom Webster to deliver the critically important sealed envelope—containing the DNA phenotype mugshot description—to Jake Cravens.

A veteran of the department, Webster was a bit of a jokester. He always liked to dress up like a jolly Santa Claus during the Christmas season. Today was no exception. He wore his badge and still carried his revolver, handcuffs, radio and nightstick on his waist. But the rest of him could have passed for Saint Nick.

Because the always-up-for-fun sheriff's deputy had a bushy white mustache, a belly-button long white beard, a thick crop of gray hair combed straight back and a wide black belt. His shirt was Christmas red and white.

"Ho, ho, ho!" he said when Coffmann put the envelope in his hand and told him how essential a piece of evidence it was. "Old Saint Nick'll get on his reindeer and go right to that newspaper man. And it'll make his day, I'm sure."

Coffmann smiled and said: "Just don't let anybody see you dropping it down the chimney. This is to be put personally in his hands. Understood?"

"Yes sir, Sheriff. Ho, ho, ho and jingle bells rock, Merry Christmas and may you catch that SOB murderer!"

Back at the *News-Journal*, Donald Mink had been alerted that his work on the profile sketch was not complete.

"I have to go now, love," he spoke into the phone to his new friend, a transgender florist he'd met online. "They've got me going to some kind of stuffy meeting in my boss' office. Lucky me."

Minutes later, Cravens shared with Lowery and Mink the potential power of DNA phenotyping. He told them the forensics experts were convinced it could help reveal a suspect's face.

His eyes rarely leaving his freshly painted fingernails, Mink listened politely, nodding occasionally to signify to his superiors that he understood. He asked them if he might be permitted to file a complaint against a reporter who had been bothering him.

"Bothering you how?" Lowery asked. "Because we take pride in having a safe, inclusive workplace here at the *News-Journal*, and I'm sure I speak for Mr. Cravens when I say that. Isn't that right, Mr. Cravens?"

Cravens had never personally liked Donald Mink, thinking of him as a bit of a dweeb, and had taken grief in Summer's Rest for hiring him. But he had kept him on the payroll because of his unusual skills. Thus, the publisher grudgingly acknowledged his liberal editor's sentiment about inclusiveness.

Then he asked his graphic artist to elaborate on what he meant by being bothered.

Donald toyed with his body piercings, crinkled his face and squirmed in his chair. "I mean, sir, that they treat me like I'm some kind of pervert," he whimpered. "Like I don't belong. Like I should be wearing a scarlet letter. And I feel like I'm always under a microscope. Maybe I should resign."

"We all respect you very much," was the only response Lowery could think of.

"And think of you as one of our most esteemed employees," Cravens added. "That's why we know you can help our good sheriff solve this horrific murder case."

Sensing that Donald was coming around, Lowery said, "We're depending on you. You are the best graphic artist in these parts. Better'n anybody this side of Knoxville."

"Our serial killer's as good as caught, thanks to you, Donald," Cravens chimed in. He stood up and bear-hugged his most detested employee. "And if they catch this guy, rest assured there'll be a little something extra on your next paycheck."

Feeling better about how he stood at the newspaper and about a potential bonus in his pay, Donald thanked them and returned to his work cubicle. Not long after that, he had the contents of the envelope delivered by "Santa Claus' deputy sheriff," as people in the newsroom dubbed him.

Donald read and reread the DNA phenotype profile description.

Then he looked at his sketch of the suspect. He had been almost entirely spot on with how the killer might look.

Except, according to the DNA genetic markers, the man they were looking for was not just tall, but very tall—more than six and one-half feet tall—and his face was not just thin; it was abnormally thin. And while he was a Caucasian, he had a nose almost as wide as that of an African-American. The shape of his jawbone would be round and wide. But his chin was almost pointed—jutting out prominently.

The algorithm for the genetic markers predicted that he was about 38 years old, had dark brown eyes that were closer together than normal, brown hair and that his skin, while white, was dark in tone. *Musta' been a melungeon in the woodpile,* Donald surmised.

And one more thing: this was a massive Big Foot like human being. He weighed close to 300 pounds, with huge feet and hands, strong bones and muscles that probably rippled.

I can definitely work with this. It'll be like putting flesh on his bones, Donald thought. Then he looked again at the sketch he'd already created. It almost creeped him out about how close he already had come to capturing a likeness of the killer.

Chapter 17
Emma Della

The *News-Journal* published Donald's sketch, along with a short article explaining the DNA science and FBI profiling behind the artist's work. It appeared prominently on the front page, above the fold, so that everyone could see it on the newspaper racks and through the window of the paper's vending machines.

True to the excited publisher's prediction, sales of the newspaper increased substantially. And not only for the day the initial drawing and article appeared, but for the subsequent five days. Because of the paper's skyrocketing circulation—tied to its unrelenting coverage of the murders of Hazel Eula Haynes, Gracie Spencer and Carrie Belle Harris—Cravens mulled an advertising rate increase.

The idea didn't sit well with editor Lowery. "Isn't that just capitalizing on the misery of these three distraught families, Mr. Cravens?" he asked. "Plus, I thought we had a firewall between news and advertising. We're reporting the news and serving the public. Seems like that should be our mission—not to profit from someone else's unfortunate circumstances."

Cravens exploded: "The purpose of a newspaper—or the free press, for that matter—IS TO MAKE MONEY! Didn't they teach you anything in that fancy journalism school?!"

He reminded his young editor of all the bad news regularly published in the *News-Journal.* The publisher noted that the paper ran the public record every week—and it was chock full of the names of people arrested for shoplifting, driving while under the influence, assault, violating probation and otherwise running afoul of the law.

"With all due respect, sir, that just seems somehow to be different.

And we don't raise our advertising rates just because we have a full page of people arrested for shoplifting or failing to pay their child support."

Cravens got right up into his editor's face, so close that his spit sprayed the nose of his listener. "You need to remember one thing about journalism. GOOD NEWS IS NO NEWS! And we've got a situation here, with this serial killer, where it's our solemn obligation to inform the community AND keep our newspaper strong. We can only do that when we make money! Do I make myself clear, Mr. Lowery?"

The defeated editor knew it was senseless to argue any more. He said "yes sir" and shriveled back to his office.

Meanwhile, across town, at the busiest fastfood restaurant in Summer's Rest, a young woman with Down syndrome went about her daily work of wiping down the tables, refilling customers' drinks, sweeping the floor and emptying the trash.

Her name was Emma Della Davis, and she had become beloved by many a fast food customer at one of the town's most popular eating places.

"Hello, Emma Della. You're sure looking nice today," a customer complimented her when she flashed him a big smile.

Emma Della, 30, had begun working at McDonald's after her graduation from a special education high school. The restaurant's manager at the time had been raising a child with Down syndrome of his own. So when his close friends Ray and Maxine Davis had asked him to give their daughter a chance, he had readily agreed.

Shorter and with a flatter face, bigger tongue, thinner upper lip and shorter nose than those she served at the restaurant, that didn't stop her from radiating happiness and cheerfulness. Nor did it stop her from being one of her employer's most reliable, conscientious workers.

At first, some customers had been offput, encountering an employee with Down syndrome. But they had come around when they saw how hard she worked. She was proud of her McDonald's smock, covered with badges and an "I'm lovin' it" nameplate, and always made sure her uniform was cleaned and pressed. For that matter, if you were going by clothes alone, Emma Della was "the sharpest knife in the drawer," as one of her fellow employees said.

"Ain't she just the sweetest little thing you ever saw?" a grandmotherly, blue-haired lady remarked when Emma Della mopped the floor. "And I'll bet her family adores her."

McDonald's employees came and went, but Emma Della stayed. And soon, she began working behind the counter—running the fryolator and putting customers' orders on their trays. Framed certificates touting her as "Employee of the Month" hung on one wall of the eating place.

But regardless of what she did—whether it was wiping and swiping throughout the eating area or making sure customers had their drink cups full—Emma Della made a lasting impression.

So enduring that some people, meaning well but possibly also offending her close family, would refer to her as "Twenty-one." No one seemed to know exactly who came up with the moniker "Twenty-one," but conventional wisdom was that it derived from Emma Della having an extra chromosome 21—instead of the usual 46 chromosomes that others had.

"She's just who she is. She's a unique child of God and we all love her," said a man in a hooded jacket sucking a chocolate shake from a straw. "Plus, she doesn't know a stranger. She treats everybody the same."

Three teenagers sat at another table, paying Emma Della no mind when she asked them if they needed refills. Their heads down and oblivious to those around them, they were entranced by their smartphones. Texting, Instagram, Snapchat and Facebook had their full attention.

Nearby, a middle-aged man in a plaid red and green Christmas shirt munched on his fries and gave Emma Della a Donald Trump thumbs-up when she offered him a complimentary copy of the *News-Journal.* Strapped to his waist was a holstered pistol—something you had begun seeing more often since the three recent murders.

In a corner booth, a young couple munched on their quarter-pounders and tried to remain inconspicuous. Each of their faces was pocked with scabs and sores—a telltale clue of their meth habits.

When Emma Della asked if they needed anything, they brushed her off. Her language skills and articulation were not the best, so many of the restaurant's patrons couldn't quite understand her. Even after repeated attempts at communication, Emma Della struggled. On the other hand, she seemed to understand quite well.

"That gal understands a lot more of what we say than what we understand from her," Mona Parker said. "But I don't care. She's the most precious kid on this planet."

Mona, a perpetual gum-chewing assistant manager, had worked closely with Emma Della for three years. She looked after her at work and took her shopping at Walmart on the weekends. She was Emma Della's constant ray of sunshine. And she always had her back.

At the counter, two people had just placed their orders. The man, maybe a college student, wore wrinkled pajama bottoms and a dirty sweatshirt with words printed on it that said "IF YOU DON'T LIKE MY DOG, I DON'T LIKE YOU." Behind him was a haggard-looking woman in baggy jeans, a pleated red jacket, long faded blue shirt dangling below her waist, and matching red Crocs.

Just another busy day at McDonald's, a place some folks called the home of the "Liars Table" because so many locals came here not just to eat but to gossip and catch up with the latest news.

"Emma Della, you're doing a good job!" her shift manager barked from behind the counter. His name was Clyde Bradley and he, like Emma Della, had started at McDonald's right out of high school. Partly because turnover was high there and the pay was just slightly higher than the minimum wage—but also because he always showed up and did his job well—Clyde had risen quickly through the ranks at the restaurant. He took a personal interest in Emma Della's welfare and couldn't bear the thought that someone would ever insult her.

Not that many people belittled Emma Della, but a tiny minority of them did. If Clyde Bradley got wind of that, he was the first to invite them to take their business elsewhere. But he would first remind them that, but for the grace of God, they, too, could be like Emma Della. "She's not a walking disability," he had often said. "She's a person and we need to focus on what she can do, not on what she can't."

Such talk maybe didn't win over every hard hearted, rude customer. But it made Clyde Bradley feel better about himself. "Please make sure that everyone that wants one—gets a copy of today's newspaper, Emma Della," Clyde shouted out to his favorite employee while he worked on next week's work schedule.

"I do dat," Emma Della responded.

With an armful of newspapers—bulging with advertising supplements—she gradually made her way around the dining area.

"You want a paper, suh?" she asked.

"May-yam, would you like to read da nuze-paper?"

Most of the customers she offered a free paper to politely declined—a sign of the times of so many getting their news on their smartphones from social media. But a few people, mostly older Boomers, eagerly took her up on the offer of a free copy of the *News-Journal*, and some even offered to pay her.

"No suh. No may-yam," she'd say. "Dis be part of muh job."

And so it went throughout her shift. Emma Della cleaned, swept, emptied, refilled and fried. And she did it all, hardly saying a word.

At the end of her four-hour work shift, she retreated to a back corner of the dining room and enjoyed a tall soft drink, hamburger and fries. She would linger there for about 30 minutes until her parents picked her up.

Only today, something about Emma Della's after-work routine was different.

There she sat in her favorite booth—reading the *News-Journal*. And not just anything in the *News-Journal*. Her little callused fingers ran across the words written by editor Dudley Lowery—about the profile of the wanted serial killer. Emma Della mumbled to herself as she read.

And she couldn't seem to take her oddly shaped, smaller-than-normal eyes off the sketch drawn by Donald Mink. "I tink' I seen dis' man!" she yelled. In the excitement of the moment, she spilled her soft drink all over her lap.

People stopped eating and drinking for a few seconds. A few craned their necks toward the little animated woman who was causing a stir.

No one said anything.

And then Emma Della, standing up and ketchup from her french fries dribbling from the side of her mouth, blurted it out again: "I tink' I seen dis' man!"

Chapter 18
A Break in the Case

High Sheriff Ethan Coffmann had decided to escape from his office once again—a routine that was becoming more common of late. There had been the anonymous calls from those demanding that he resign. There had been whispers of discontent from some of his deputies who were beginning to lose confidence in him. There had been shouts from visitors at the jail, wondering why their loved ones were locked up for seemingly minor crimes when a ghoulish serial killer roamed freely.

And there had been the interminable stream of letters to the editor in the *News-Journal*—most of them signed because the newspaper rarely published an anonymous letter.

"We didn't elect you to drink coffee and arrest shoplifters and pack your jail with deadbeat dads," one writer complained. "Besides, how in tarnation is a man supposed to pay his child support if he's behind bars? Why don't you get off your no-good rear end and find that murderer?"

Another writer wondered how the sheriff could sleep at night "given what horror is afflicting our little community."

But the sharpest and most hurtful, for the high sheriff, rebuke came from an elderly lady who wrote of the very recent blockbuster arrest of an ex-cop in California. After decades of trying to nail the man known as the Golden State Killer, police announced they had finally caught the person responsible for killing 12 people and sexually assaulting at least 45 women. The letter writer pointed out the eerie similarity between Joseph James Angelo— arrested by California police on charges of killing/raping all those innocents in the 1970s and 1980s—and Taylor County's own High Sheriff Ethan Coffmann. Both, she wrote, had law enforcement backgrounds. Both were military veterans. In the case of Mr. Angelo, a police sketch artist had helped play a big role in nabbing the long sought-after suspect.

"And just look, will you, at the size of that suspect depicted by the *News-Journal*'s own artist?!" she exclaimed in her letter. "Could that not be our very own High Sheriff Ethan Coffmann?"

As for the sheriff's combat Marine heroism—which had been front and center in his last campaign—one writer questioned that. "How do we even know you fought?" the skeptic asked. "Because you've betrayed our trust in every other way. You've got to be the lyingnest, no-good-for-nothin' sheriff in the history of East Tennessee."

Another writer declared: "God, the U.S. Flag, Guns, Donald Trump and RECALL SHERIFF ETHAN COFFMANN!"

Publisher Jake Cravens told his good friend that he hated to run some of the letters but the paper had no choice. "Because otherwise, we'd be accused of a cover-up," Cravens said. "And besides, any newspaper worth its salt provides a forum for public opinion."

Coffmann tried to take it all in stride, reminding himself that all the public vitriol came with his job.

But as for Jake Cravens' high and mighty notions about what a newspaper was supposed to do, he thought his old friend was more full of it than a constipated turkey.

Today, as he cruised the main drag of town, snow and ice made moving about difficult. An arctic blast had brought the white stuff, and wind chills were in the single digits. Icy glaze coated the giant sycamore trees near the covered bridge. And beneath the bridge, the picturesque little waterfall, almost the width of the river, had turned into a sheet of solid ice. Overhead, a formation of honking Canada geese broke the wintry stillness.

The sheriff drove slowly, hoping that most folks would have the good sense to stay inside—and off the road—today.

But it wasn't to be. At the main intersection outside Walmart, the busiest stop light in the city limits, a three-car collision had blocked the main entrance to the largest store in Summer's Rest. Irate Christmas shoppers were getting impatient. A couple of them had started blowing their horns. One bundled-up man had gotten out of his car, was pacing back and forth and seemed to be yelling obscenities into his cell phone. He flashed the bird toward someone behind him.

Just part of the daily grind of life here.

Coffmann could hear emergency sirens in the distance, so no need, he figured, to call dispatch.

A call came over his police radio. "Taylor County One, Taylor County One, come in."

"Taylor County One here," Coffmann responded.

"The manager of McDonald's wants you to come over there soon as possible. Says he's got someone at the restaurant who can help us I.D. our murder suspect."

Coffmann's heart sped up. He gripped the steering wheel more tightly and activated the Crown Vic's overhead flashing blue lights and siren.

He made a quick 180 at the Walmart accident scene and headed to McDonald's.

The fast food outlet was about empty as dinnertime approached. But in an hour, the place would be packed with people hungry for their Big Macs, fries and one-dollar large Mickey D cups of tea.

"What's the latest, Sheriff Coffmann?" McDonald's shift manager Clyde Bradley asked when the county's chief law enforcement officer entered the dining area.

Coffmann always found such a question trite. So he answered with his standard "just trying to put one foot in front of another and catch the bad guys."

The manager smiled and asked him to accompany him to a side seating area.

There in a booth, a newspaper spread out on the table in front of her, sat Emma Della Davis. Her normally impeccably clean uniform bore the stains of a spilled drink.

Coffmann noticed right away that she seemed nervous. She looked down, as if she were afraid, when he approached her. Then she shaded her rapidly blinking eyes with her left hand.

She's obviously upset, he thought.

After introducing him to Emma Della, who extended her smaller than normal right hand to the sheriff, the manager got right to it.

"Emma Della here is one of our best employees. She's been our Employee of the Month several times. We all love her."

Coffmann listened politely and told Emma Della that she should be proud of herself. *But what's this got to do with my murder investigation?*

"Emma Della, can you tell the sheriff what you told me about that man you say you know from the newspaper?"

At first, she said nothing. She wrung her hands, crinkled her mouth and shuffled in her chair. Then she picked up the newspaper, ran her fingers across the article written by editor Lowery and pointed to the DNA-based sketch of the suspect. "I know dis man. I seen him! I 'member him!" she said.

"Tell the sheriff where you saw him, Emma Della," her manager said gently.

"He was sittin' by da nap-Keans," she said. "Over dere in dat booth."

She pointed to a table in the main area of the dining room near the drink and ice machine.

The sheriff didn't know what to make of it. *Testimony from an alleged eyewitness with a mental disability—how credible would that be? And testimony, at that, based on a sketch derived from still-in-its-infancy DNA science. Let's say, just for the sake of argument, she did see him? So what? What would that prove? And where was the man now?*

"There's more," the manager said.

"Emma Della, tell the sheriff what you told me about what happened that day when you saw this man."

"I took da trash out to da dummm-ster. And I seen him get in his truck." Emma Della's language skills were not the best but the sheriff, all ears now, could understand her. He leaned forward a few inches so he wouldn't miss a word.

"Tell the sheriff about that truck, Emma Della."

She proceeded to describe to them, in broken and choppy but understandable language, how the red truck "had something like you'd see on top of a deer's head on da front of it" and "it had a sticker on the back of it about one of those ghost things."

The manager translated. "Deer antlers on the front grill of a red pickup truck, Sheriff, and a Zombie bumper sticker or decal on the back."

The sheriff's heart quickened again. He got up to leave, but manager Clyde Bradley motioned for him to sit back down.

He told Coffmann that Emma Della had one more important thing to tell him.

"He was sittin' behind dat woman in the newspaper," she said.

"Which woman?" the sheriff asked.

"Dat one here," she said, trembling while she pointed to a picture of the killer's first murder victim. The photos and names of all three victims ran beneath the profile story and sketch. The picture she had selected was that of Hazel Eula Haynes."

Bradley clarified: "She used to come in here all the time. Would have breakfast and coffee with her church lady friends. We even got so we gave them the coffee on the house. A sweet bunch of women."

Emma Della, glancing out the window, noticed that her parents had arrived to take her home. "Me has to go now," she said. "But I be back tomorrow. I promise."

When she had exited, the sheriff turned his attention back to Bradley.

He asked him straight up if Emma Della could be believed.

"She's never lied to us, Sheriff. In fact, I think she's incapable of telling a lie.

"She may be SIMPLE—as some insensitive folks say—but we love her just the same. She's not got a bad bone or a lazy bone in that little body of hers, and she's truthful to the core."

"And you would swear that under oath in a court of law?" the sheriff asked.

"I would in a heartbeat, sir, and so would everyone else who works with her."

Back at the sheriff's office, two people—Jake Cravens and Dudley Lowery—had been waiting for him. "We know something's cookin',

Sheriff," Cravens said. "Cause a little birdie told us you had a very important encounter over at McDonald's."

Editor Lowery said nothing.

The sheriff told them to stay seated in the waiting room while he attended to some pressing business.

But the publisher and his editor barged into the sheriff's office anyway.

Cravens was angry: "There ain't no secrets in a small town, Ethan! You know that. Now tell us what you found out at McDonald's."

Lowery was more diplomatic. He struck a conciliatory tone: "What he's saying, sir, is that our newspaper has been cooperating with you whole heartedly to help you find this serial killer. And now we respectfully want to be informed of the latest development in the case."

"You'll know more when I know more!" the under-siege sheriff growled. "The last thing I want to deal with right now is the *News-Journal*."

The publisher grew more insistent, saying: "In that case, Ethan, we'll make it a point to interview every person who works at that McDonald's, starting with the manager and down to whoever scrubs the bathrooms or carries out the trash.

"There's an old saying in journalism," Cravens added. "The truth emerges from many voices. Another saying's that three people can keep a secret if two of 'em's dead. Rest assured, we won't stop till we find out the truth of what you learned today at that restaurant.

"And by the way, we'll be running a front-page opinion piece about how the elected sheriff of our fair county—the very same sheriff that we've been trying to help solve these heinous crimes—has now refused to talk to us."

"Dammit, we got a lead!" Coffmann screamed, "but I haven't even had a chance to report it to the TBI or FBI."

The blood coursing through his veins like that of a long distance runner, Cravens pressed his old friend for more.

The sheriff declined, saying the case was "under investigation" and thus information about it was exempt from disclosure, per Tennessee's freedom of information law.

"Off-the-record, then, deep background, not for publication, professional courtesy, pillow talk—whatever you want to call it, Sheriff—share with us what you found out today. You have my word of honor that I'll swear on my mother's grave that we'll keep what you tell us extremely confidential."

Coffmann caved, reluctantly, and told them what he'd learned from Emma Della.

Cravens was astonished.

"You mean that little retard that cleans tables and refill's people's drinks? THAT Emma Della. You're basing your whole case on the word of a retard?"

That hit a nerve. "She is not a retard Jake! She happens to be one of their most valued and loyal employees. She has a disability, and so do you with your big mouth!"

The publisher wasn't fazed: "So how do you know she's telling the truth? What's to prove she's on the up and up?"

"You print thousands of words every day in your newspaper, Jake, and how in God's name do you know *those* are truthful?"

"Because we're professionals and news is usually one of two things, Ethan. Somebody says something, or something happens. With regard to the former, I believe we do a heckuva job vetting our sources. And when somebody tells us something particularly shocking or titillating, we cross-check that information with another source. We do not just run with it because it's exciting."

"Yeah, you're the esteemed guardians of the First Amendment. And they made it the first Amendment because it's the most important freedom we have. I've heard all that drivel before, Jake.

"Just give me a break and let me do my job, will you?" the exasperated sheriff pleaded.

"We'll give you 24 hours to deal with this lead," Cravens said. "But then we can't sit on it any longer. It'll be on the front page of Sunday's paper. That's because the public has a right to know."

"And you're the righteous surrogate of the public, correct?" the sheriff responded sarcastically.

Then he lit into Cravens with a vengeance. "You realize that if you print this story and the murderer sees it, he'll most likely hightail it out of Taylor County quicker'n Pat joined the army. But if you're smart about it, and you truly have the public interest at heart, you'll let us do our job—without compromising our investigation."

Cravens thought about that for a moment. "So if the *News-Journal* sits on this story, what'll the newspaper get out of it?"

The sheriff promised him an exclusive interview if and when they took a suspect into custody.

"Word of honor, Ethan?" Cravens asked.

"You have my solemn word, Jake."

David Patrick Jackson III turned up the volume of his radio when he heard the hit 1960s song by the Beach Boys.

Well East Coast girls are hip
I really dig those styles they wear
And the Southern girls with the way they talk
They knock me out when I'm down there ...
I wish they all could be California girls! ...

Reclining in an old ratty chair that looked to be on the brink of falling apart, Jackson hummed along to the words and beat of one of his all-time favorite songs. It was a tune that stuck in his mind the rest of this wintry, fiercely cold afternoon. *What am I doing here in this godforsaken frozen wasteland?*

He pictured himself frolicking on a beach—maybe playing volleyball or sharing a few cool beers—with golden tanned, bikini-clad beauties. Or riding the blue ocean waves. Or building sandcastles with a California blonde goddess who'd later take him home with her.

Suddenly the Beach Boys song was over and the smartass DJ began chatting with a caller. "How cold is it up your way?" the DJ asked.

Replied the man on the other end of the phone, who described himself as a hillbilly and *mighty proud of it:* "It's so dad gummed cold that when I let my dog out this morning to do its business, his pee froze in the air!"

The DJ laughed heartily.

A woman called in and said where she lived—on the outer limits of the county—they'd had six inches of snow yesterday, but it was all gone by today.

"So it's gone so fast?" the DJ asked skeptically. "How could so much snow have disappeared so quickly—in just one day?"

Without missing a beat, the woman told him they'd had a ferocious wind "and the snow done blowed itself to death!"

Gut-splitting laughter from the DJ.

For David Patrick Jackson III, however, the exchange confirmed just how foreboding and backward a place he had moved to. He had never even heard of Summer's Rest or Taylor County, Tennessee, before he arrived here, and now it seemed to him like the end of the earth.

"A Friendly, Lovely, Little Town," the sign boasted when you entered the city limits. Another sign at the other edge of town described Summer's Rest as "A Place for Families, Church, Work and Relaxation." But all of that was just so much promotional drivel for the man police so avidly sought.

Nothing but a big fat lie! he thought. *Just a place for a buncha' old church-going, Bible-thumpin' pill poppers puttin' on airs. And why am I staying in this ice cold hell hole? What's keeping me here?*

So he decided then and there that, within a week or two, he'd pack up and move to California. And if his old Chevy pickup truck broke down on the way out there, he'd just hitchhike.

The blonde beauties, sun and beaches were waiting for him, and *besides, they say it's all happening out west. The smartest, richest and best looking babes in the world live in California.*

On that pleasant thought, he decided to pop a couple of pills, kick back and dream of better days in sunnier, warmer places and *get away from this polar vortex, whatever tha' hell that is.*

That miserable prison in West Tabor City, North Carolina—where a chunk of his life had been swallowed up—seemed light years away. But increasingly, of late, he had the nagging feeling that if he stayed in East Tennessee he'd end up back behind bars. Because somehow, someway—David Patrick Jackson III feared—the police had a way of getting on to you.

For that matter, it seemed to be that wherever he drove these last few weeks he noticed the lurking presence of law enforcement.

Cops, deputy sheriffs, state troopers, constables. They lay in wait in marked or unmarked cars in church and school parking lots, behind big trees or rocks, in private driveways, around the next bend in the road. For David Patrick Jackson III, it appeared that East Tennessee had an abundance of police officers—many of them likely bored and all of them chomping at the bit to make their quota of arrests. *And wouldn't they do just about anything to land the big one?*

However, no need to worry about that right now, he thought. His fear dissolved into numbness as the pain pills began to take effect.

Oblivious, as he lost consciousness, to what he feared was inevitable: a heavy snow, howling wind and icy, bone-chilling temperatures.

Chapter 19
A Bird's Eye View

The following night over dinner, Ethan Coffmann and his wife Laura had a lot to talk about. Laura's news was that their oldest son had decided to pursue medical school after graduation from college. Youngest son, a junior at Summer's Rest High School, had joined the staff of the school newspaper.

"He really loves journalism and current events," the sheriff's wife said. "Especially sports journalism. His dream is to be a reporter for ESPN."

Her husband, who had skipped lunch that day because of his work load, helped himself to another big spoonful of mashed potatoes, then slathered them with Laura's delicious homemade gravy. He smiled but said nothing.

Suddenly, his wife got up and threw her napkin down on the table. "That's all you think about, isn't it?! That murder investigation!! It's ruining our lives!" She clutched her elbows tightly and threw her head back.

He stood up and hugged her. He whispered in her ear. "Can you keep a secret, honey?" he asked.

She wasn't game. "If it's about all those murders and people that keep spewing venom in the newspaper, I don't want to hear it!"

"We might have gotten a break in the case. But I'm swearing you to secrecy. Nobody, except for me and a witness and the *News-Journal* publisher and his editor is privy."

"You know that fat man's a gossiper and can't keep anything out of his paper. But if you can confide in him, well, I'm your wife and I have a right to know ..."

He told her about Emma Della and what she had shared with her manager and him.

"I know that girl!" Laura beamed. "She's adorable. And her parents are just the sweetest people you can imagine. Her mother and I organized the bake sale for homeless veterans."

Her husband countered, "Everybody seems to have a good feeling about Emma Della, but can we take what she says to the bank?"

His wife kissed him lightly and put her arms around him—her fragrance filling his senses. Then she spoke lightly. "Emma Della's an angel sent to you from God. He wants you to catch the bad guy and she's helping make that happen.

"God bless Emma Della Davis!" said Laura, tears of happiness beginning to flow.

They looked deeply into each other eyes—for the first time in many weeks. Ethan squeezed her closer to him. He delighted in the feel of her body, her scent, her caressing the back of his neck.

"The dishes can wait," said Laura, giggling.

They walked hand in hand to the bedroom, their other hands fumbling with buttons and zippers. Quickly, they undressed each other—which in their early married years had been a fiery turn-on for them—and tumbled giddily into bed. And in their king-sized bed they stayed, panting and then resting and then making love again before dozing off. They were spent and slept enwrapped in each other's arms and legs.

Ethan Coffmann didn't dream that night of killing or victims or DNA. Instead, he lost consciousness in an aura of roses, warmth and love. And there, in that ether dream land, somewhere in a billowy cloud above him, was an angelic, glowing, smiling Emma Della Davis. "It'll be ok," she softly said. "It's almost over."

Nine hours later, they'd showered with each other—sensuously sudsing up and shampooing each other's hair, which they hadn't done for many months.

Then they toweled off, dressed and vowed never again to grow so far apart.

Laura made her husband a pot of coffee and warmed some biscuits in the oven. "I just believe with all my heart that this is going to be a good day," she predicted, kissing him.

One tongue again began exploring the other tongue. They stood up, hugged, glanced toward the bedroom and smiled. Laura untied her apron. He loosened his belt.

Then the phone rang.

It was Deputy Roby Cooper. Knowing that his boss didn't like to be bothered at home, unless it was extremely urgent, he first apologized for calling so early.

"It's all right, Roby," said the sheriff, taking another sip of his hot brew. "Just tell me what's up." He cupped the phone to his neck and began refastening his belt.

The deputy proceeded to say that there were two men in suits at the sheriff's office. One was from the FBI. The other from the TBI. "They say it's important that they talk to you, sir. I offered to patch them through to you on the phone, but they want an in-person meeting."

"Tell 'em to hold their horses. I'll be there in 15 minutes," Coffmann said.

"Honey, hold that thought. I'm gone," said the sheriff, straightening his collar and going out the door. "Tell the boys we'll all go out to dinner tonight. And tell 'em I'm proud of 'em!"

On his way in, Coffmann rolled to a stop and lowered his window when he saw a homeless man shivering in a ragged blanket next to the covered bridge entrance. The 135-year-old historic bridge had been closed to traffic years ago, and engineers had recently warned that it was leaning. But some folks persisted in ignoring the cross-post barriers and walking across it. Coffmann surmised that on such a deathly cold winter night, the man had taken refuge inside the bridge—to shelter himself from the wind.

"Hey, Walt!" The sheriff shouted to the old man. He had guessed who the refugee might be but saw, as the man roused, that he had been right. Walter Dorgan refused to stay in the shelter at the mission for reasons he kept to himself.

"Where's the rest of your belongings?" the sheriff asked.

"Over yonder," the bedraggled man said, pointing toward the inside of the bridge.

"Go get 'em and get in the back seat," Coffmann said.

The old man, wearing a tattered Army field jacket, replied, "You arresting me, Sheriff?"

"No, Walter, I'm giving you a warm place to stay and hot food—in a cell in my jail. And then we'll call Social Services. Now get in. You'll die out here if you don't."

"Much obliged, Sheriff!"

Once he got to his office, Ethan Coffmann met with special agent Ron Hansen of the FBI and agent Charles Perry of the TBI. Both were immaculately dressed—in dark blue and black suits, laundered white shirts with cuff links, crisp, brightly colored ties and shiny black shoes.

The federal and state boys get paid good, Coffmann thought.

Hansen spoke first: "Sheriff, we have an issue to discuss. The FBI and the TBI is turning down your request for helicopter air support. We simply do not think that choppers will be able to find that red pickup truck. They'd have way too much terrain to search, and besides, when you put two crew members in each chopper—one person as the pilot and the other as a spotter—the cost is extremely prohibitive."

Coffmann, who had been sitting down, sprang up quickly from his desk. He clinched his fists.

"What do you mean?! I have 15 deputies and 10 constables. So how in the world are we supposed to be able to search 350 square miles of mountains, ridges, valleys and housing developments? Not to mention God only knows how many trailer parks and off-the-grid campgrounds. *We plain and simple cannot do it!* Meanwhile, we have a serial killer on our hands—one who we strongly believe drives an old red pickup truck. A truck with some sort of Zombie sticker on its back bumper or rear glass and deer antlers—if they're still there—on its front grill.

"We need help from the state and from the federal government finding that truck. Because this guy's going to strike again! Strange thing to me the feds and our esteemed commander-in-chief can spend billions of dollars fighting terrorists and billions more, it appears, on a useless wall running along hundreds of miles of our southern border. All that and they can't spare us a few choppers!"

This time, special agent Perry spoke. "Sheriff, the honorable governor of the state of Tennessee—Francis H. Blanton—feels your pain. That's why he's dispatching 10 UAV's to search every nook and cranny of Taylor County."

"UAV?" Coffmann asked, puzzled. "What the hell is a UAV?"

"Unmanned Aerial Vehicle," the FBI agent said. "You probably know them as drones."

"You mean like they use in Iran and Afghanistan to pinpoint the enemy? To show our pilots where to drop their bombs?"

"They're increasingly being used in law enforcement and for other purposes, Sheriff," special agent Hansen explained.

He went on to describe how coastal communities employ drones to scour the ocean—near beaches—for sharks; how forestry services use them to help find lost hikers; and how drones have come to be used to help catch illegal aliens trying to sneak across the U.S. border.

"Think of them as unmanned aerial robots, flying at high altitude, with computers in them," Hansen said. "Computers with Artificial Intelligence programmable software that's connected to our mainframe computer at the National Crime Information Center."

The agent explained that there'd be no worries with the solar-powered, high-resolution camera-equipped drones making people scared or suspicious, given that they'd be flying at an altitude of 20,000 feet. From that altitude, he noted, the drone's video surveillance camera could detect objects as little as about a half-foot long. One of the drones could observe a 10-square mile land mass area in only a few seconds.

And even if, say, a local pilot happened to spot one of the UAVs, the agent said, authorities could always tell a white lie. Something to the effect that the flying robots were being dispatched to more closely map terrain not easily seen by satellites in outer space.

"Geeky stuff," the sheriff said.

"Yes, definitely, and so much more cost efficient than manned helicopters," said Perry, smiling. "Our tech people will program them to fly in a grid pattern, back and forth, so that every square foot of your county is scoured with their video cameras—sort of like a search and rescue team combs the woods, back and forth, looking for a lost child."

"So how'll they find that red pickup truck?" the sheriff asked.

Agent Hansen said the video surveillance camera on the drones could be programmed to recognize and flag certain shapes, colors or objects—pickup trucks, for example—and to automatically store and retrieve those digital images for closer analysis at the NCIC.

"And there's absolutely no problem with a drone violating a person's privacy," Perry said. "We can legally take a picture of whatever's in plain view. In other words, anything is fair game for our video surveillance that a normal, everyday passerby person could easily see with his own two eyes."

"I get it," the sheriff said. "What you're saying is that your little electronic gizmo can't aim its camera toward an open bathroom window."

"Exactly," Hansen said. "But just about everything else—again, that's in plain sight—that we can get a bird's eye view of, we can shoot video of it.

"If your suspect's truck is out there, Sheriff, we'll find it. Because if a drone can find a shark, a terrorist or a lost hiker, it can find a red pickup truck. And once we find it, we'll give you a call. From there, you'll take over. Should be a piece of cake."

Coffmann asked where, exactly, the NCIC experts would be analyzing the drone video.

"It'll be in a packed-with-electronic-gear basement at NCIC headquarters in Washington, D.C., sir," Hansen clarified.

"So what's the downside to all this drone stuff?" the stunned sheriff asked.

"That would be the tons of data our technical people will have to wade through," Hansen said. "Think about it: even if the drone camera software is programmed to alert our technical experts to objects that look like red pickup trucks, that'll translate to a lot of alerts. Just imagine how many such vehicles there are in your county."

The sheriff had visions of a giant dark room full of computer monitors, topographical grid boards and the latest technological wizardry—all being manned by FBI geeks, sipping on coffee, in white lab coats. Or maybe they were nerds with earbuds in shorts, t-shirts and tennis shoes? *But so be it,* he thought. *If it takes an airborne robot and computer techies to find our bad guy's truck, I'm all in.*

Chapter 20
Things Unknown in the Sky

A week after the 10 drones, equipped with the latest video surveillance technology, began traversing the skies above Taylor County, Tennessee, 911 dispatchers began receiving sightings of UFOs.

The solar-powered drones flew high and they flew silently, but a few eagle-eyed local stargazers had spotted them. They couldn't quite make out what kind of aerial phenomena they were. They had never seen anything like them. And that was enough to trigger a surge of reports that captured the public's imagination.

Compounding the interest in "whatever it is up there," as one local resident put it, were recent national news reports of a couple of Navy pilots spotting an unidentified flying object (UFO) several years ago. The pilot had said the mysterious object—which could turn and elevate or lower itself at warp speed— was unlike anything he'd ever seen.

Also making the news bigtime was a strange interstellar asteroid the size of a football field that had originated from another galaxy. Scientists had been monitoring the big chunk of mass for alien signals. The mere mention that our planet might have intelligent visitors from another world was more than enough to fuel excitement, and fear, in the mountains of East Tennessee.

Publisher Jake Cravens, aware that the so-called unknown flying objects were surveillance drones, got as much mileage out of the story as possible.

"All this UFO mania in our community is a newspaperman's dream!" he boasted to his editor. "We've got to play it for all it's worth."

"But boss, didn't you say they were only drones trying to pinpoint the vehicle driven by that serial killer?" editor Dudley Lowery asked.

Undeterred, Cravens said, "Never let the truth get in the way of a good story, young man! And just hope and pray that people keep all this UFO fever alive. Readers love to imagine that we are not alone in this big wide universe. If you don't believe that, look at the success of all those Star Wars movies. And the Spielberg blockbusters—*E.T.* and *Close Encounters of the Third Kind.* People want to believe that we humans are not alone. We can't wait to make contact with little green men, or whatever they might be, from outer space."

"So what do you propose exactly that we at the *News-Journal* do?"

Cravens snapped back immediately: "Milk this story for all it's worth!"

The publisher then went on to lecture his young editor about the five topics —in the publisher's opinion, based on his "considerable real-world experience in journalism"—that a newspaper can never go wrong with in covering: Sex, money, dogs, snakes and death. "And to that list, I'd add UFOs."

"Snakes?" Lowery asked. "You mean like that rattler that killed a fundamentalist preacher up in Kentucky?"

"That's exactly what I mean!" Cravens said. "Would that that fool preacher had been tempting fate in Taylor County. But in the meantime just hope and pray that if somebody gets bit by a snake in our fair community that it's a poisonous one," said Cravens. "Makes for more drama and a better story. People thrive on reading about people bit by rattlesnakes."

A few miles outside of town, David Patrick Jackson III began planning his move. Not many bags to pack because he had brought hardly anything with him those several months ago when he relocated to East Tennessee.

But he wondered how far he'd get in his 1999 Chevy S-10 truck. The old trap had almost 200,000 miles on it, and it had started to guzzle oil. Two tires were getting bald and you had to pump the brakes to make them work. The radio and wipers only worked when they wanted to. Some no-good-for-nothing nobody—who and when he didn't know—had thrown a rock through the driver side window. He had patched the glass best he could with duct tape.

All in all, a pitiful, sorry excuse for a vehicle, he thought. *But long as it gets me outta these mountains and on my way to California, I'll be good to go.*

He also feared that bad weather was just around the corner, and so, if he were serious about pulling up stakes, he better not wait too long. The winters in East Tennessee could be brutal. Already, baby powder snow covered the tops of the mountains all around him. A gloomy gray cloudless sky seemed to promise that heavy snow was on the way. Weather forecasters had talked about single digit temperatures, the result of something called a bomb cyclone in the Northeast, due soon for Summer's Rest.

Way too cold for this old boy. Then he began humming a few bars of the "I wish they all could be California girls," Beachboys song.

At the McDonald's on a busy thoroughfare of Summer's Rest, the popular restaurant was as bustling as ever. The overcrowded parking lot had already been the scene—earlier that day—of a couple of fender benders. Every single parking space was at a premium, unless you were willing to leave your vehicle across the highway at the bank and walk to the restaurant. But the frigid, face freezing temperatures made walking a last resort. So folks battled for those precious parking spaces at McDonald's.

People had apparently taken a break from Christmas shopping to fill their bellies with Big Macs, fries, chicken nuggets, shakes and soft drinks or hot coffee. Today, the bitter cold weather dominated almost every conversation.

Peggy Sue McClinton had a scarf wrapped around her neck as she bit down into her sandwich and washed it down with a hot cup of coffee. She couldn't get over how some people "way up there in Michigan and Minnesota" strip down and took something called a "polar bear plunge."

"Why, that'd stop a bidy's heart sure as anything," said a bemused

Ralph Corby, Peggy's Sue's tablemate. He coughed up some phlegm and spat it into his napkin. Peggy Sue turned her head in disgust.

Sitting at a nearby table and overhearing them, Brenda Mays, chomped down on a French fry and chimed in, saying, "Not if you jumped into the lake naked, so you wouldn't have any wet icy clothes on when you got outta' the water and they could wrap you up in a warm blanket."

"Would you be *naked* or *nekkid*?" said Ralph, biting his lip to maintain a straight face.

"What's the difference?" Brenda asked.

"All the difference in the world, dear," he said. "*Naked* means you don't have any clothes on. *Nekkid* means you don't have any clothes on and you're *up* to somethin'!"

Sheriff Ethan Coffmann—along with Walter, the homeless man he'd picked up at the bridge a couple of days previously—entered the crowded, buzzing-with-conversation dining room. Ordinarily the sheriff of Taylor County would have been greeted by half the folks in a crowded eatery, but with the divisive issue of the so-far-fruitless search for the serial killer on the table, only a few gave him a cursory nod.

Emma Della was different. She walked over to the sheriff and his visitor and welcomed them both to "da best place to eat 'yore lunch in this parta' Tennessee."

Coffmann smiled at her and introduced Emma Della to the roughly dressed, grizzled man with him. They then went to the counter to place their orders—on the sheriff's dime.

There had been a time, Coffmann remembered nostalgically, that his money had been no good at this McDonald's. Anything he ordered had been on the house, compliments of the manager. But that all changed with the killings. People nowadays were more skittish, more cold and distant.

Still, however, the manager on duty today at Mickey D's, as the younger set called this eatery, was always pleasant enough, and that's one reason the sheriff ate here.

His cell phone rang. It was special agent Hansen, who told him that his task force had decided to deploy their drones directly over Summer's Rest, gather surveillance video from within the town's city limits and then work their way, gradually, toward the outer stretches of the county.

"We're basing our aerial search on a theory called Occam's razor, Sheriff. It's the idea that, among competing answers for what we're looking for, the most obvious, most simple answer should guide us."

Coffmann mumbled something that led Hansen to believe he hadn't explained the theory clearly enough.

He clarified: "We're searching first for where we think he's most likely to be. Because if he's been at that McDonald's, chances are he didn't drive there from too far away."

"Makes sense. But you'll still fly over the whole county, right?"

"Every square foot, Sheriff," Hansen said. "And remember, our cameras have sufficient magnification that, from 20,000 feet up in the sky, we can detect a three-year-old playing in his backyard. If that pickup truck is out there, we'll find it.

"And, as you know, we had Emma Della Davis look at hundreds of photos of pickup trucks. She picked out a red one—an old Chevy—as the one she saw the suspect get into that day when she emptied the trash.

"And not only that, we showed her every bumper sticker or decal ever made that had a Zombie logo on it. She picked out a circular one that says ZOMBIE OUTBREAK RESPONSE TEAM. So how many old red Chevy pickup trucks could have such a sticker? We got some great leads from her, Sheriff."

All that Coffmann could think was that he was glad Emma Della apparently had such a good memory—given that she'd seen the truck and the sticker for only a few seconds.

But what bothered him—and what he didn't share on the phone with the special agent—was the "so what" factor.

So what if Emma Della noticed a man who fit the profile description of the suspect sitting in a booth at McDonald's in back of the first murder victim? And so what if she recalled what kind of truck he drove that day?

A good defense attorney would make a mockery of such so-called evidence—originating, at that, from a young woman with Down syndrome who claims to have read and understood a story and recognized an artist's sketch in the newspaper, an artist's sketch that could represent any number of big mountain men in east Tennessee..

On the other hand, forensic investigators had collected several samples of DNA genetic material left at the murder scenes. Based on the analysis of that DNA, the same man had committed all three murders. That was indisputable. So it was just a matter of finding the perpetrator. Find the suspect and get a DNA cheek swab from him, and you might well have nailed your murderer.

Case closed. Suspect tried and found guilty, or maybe, in the best scenario, the suspect confesses—obviating the need for a trial. High Sheriff rides off proudly into the sunset. Wife and rest of the family are ecstatic. Local community rejoices.

But, and there's always a "but," isn't there? the sheriff realized. *Even though we might get the suspect in custody, we can't legally take a DNA cheek swab from him without arresting him. Just holding him for questioning, without an arrest or a warrant, will get us nowhere.*

In the movies or on television, police had gotten suspects to take a drink of water from a glass or to eat from a plate of food. From there, the suspect's saliva was rushed to a lab for forensic analysis. An arrest quickly ensued.

But the dire situation confronting the worried sheriff in Summer's Rest wasn't fantasy. It wasn't TV drama and it wasn't Hollywood.

Without first arresting the suspect, the U.S. Supreme Court had ruled that a law enforcement agency could not legally get a fingerprint blood sample or cheek swab sample from that suspect. In making that favorable ruling for suspects, the high court had said law enforcement considerations do not trump fears of invasion of personal privacy and false accusations.

So when we find him, we'll just arrest him, Coffmann figured. *But, again, arrest him on the basis of what?* The sheriff decided that the question would somehow take care of itself when the time arose. For now, all he could do was wait.

Wait for the drones to find that red pickup truck.

Wait for the guys in the basement of the NCIC to do their thing with that mountain of video footage.

And wait for the time when he'd have the chance to question the owner of that truck.

"Sheriff, are you ok? You don't look so good," said the homeless man who had accompanied him to the restaurant. "That little girl over there has been waving at you ever since we got here. She wants to know if she can refill our drinks. She's mighty cute, ain't she?"

High Sheriff Ethan Coffmann apologized to Walter for being so distracted. Then he walked over and cradled Emma Della Davis in his arms and thanked her for helping him.

"We're gonna find that man's truck, I promise," he told her. "And when we do, you'll be the biggest hero this town has ever had."

She smiled slightly, straightened her smock and nodded acknowledgment to the sheriff.

"I know. I know," she said.

Chapter 21
Robot Magic

Four days passed. Nothing found from the aerial cameras—except for thousands of pickup trucks, hundreds of them red or borderline reddish. None of them, however, with Zombie stickers on their rear glass or bumpers, and none with antlers on their front grills. Augmented by the full resources of the state and federal governments, one of the most intensive manhunts in the history of the Taylor County Sheriff's Department continued.

The FBI and TBI agents stayed optimistic.

"Our cameras are doing their thing—capturing 6,000 terabytes of video data every day," agent Hansen told the sheriff.

Coffmann, scratching his head, had no idea what that meant, but he sensed that it was a ton of video to analyze.

"How long's it taking to zoom in on the pickup truck images?" he asked.

Hansen said the FBI's AI robots were doing that, virtually every second. "They're mighty efficient, Sheriff." "They do in an hour what it would take a human a year to complete.

"But you might be interested to know that we've gotten video of mountain lions out there roaming in the outer reaches of your fair county. Big mean cats easily capable of killing a cow or a human lickety split."

Coffmann's office had gotten reports of sightings of such creatures in recent months, but they were nothing that could be confirmed. It was a fact, however, that mountain lions, once thought not to exist in Tennessee, had been spotted earlier in the year in the Smokey Mountains—about 100 miles west of here. And there had been unconfirmed reports of the big predators—also called cougars or panthers—being caught on film by trail cameras within a few miles of the Taylor County line.

The sheriff said he'd alert the appropriate wildlife conservation agency and the local press. *Old Jake Cravens'll have himself another blockbuster story*, he thought.

David Patrick Jackson III put the final touches on a construction job—laying tile in a bathroom of a luxury cabin.

"Cheapskate!" he groused when the rich owner paid him half of what he thought the job was worth. The ex-con had mortar and grout all over his body, and his hands and knees were raw.

"Take it or leave it," the annoyed owner said. "What you done ain't worth a cent more. I coulda' got a hunderd other people to do what you did for less."

Jackson muttered an obscenity under his breath, stuffed the cash in his shirt pocket, got in his truck, which he had a hard time starting, and headed back to his trailer. He stopped at a convenience store with a couple of gas pumps to fill up the tank and to buy some jumper cables and stock up on bottled water, bootlegged cigarettes and beanie weenies.

He was almost done with packing. *Just a few loose ends to tie up. And then I'm outta here fastern' greased lightnin'.*

A few miles south, High Sheriff Ethan Coffmann and his wife Laura had just exited the movie theatre. The sheriff, at the urging of some of his deputies, had taken the day off and spent it with his wife.

She had wanted to see a movie titled *Megan Leavey*—about a soldier in Afghanistan whose life had been saved by her beloved mine-detecting dog Rex.

A line from a tough Marine sergeant stuck in the sheriff's brain as he and Laura made their way to the coffee shop near the theatre. "They're not just dogs, Corporal Leavey. They're warriors."

The sheriff began wondering: *What if Duke, the black lab mix owned by the late Carrie Belle Powers, wasn't just an ordinary dog? What if he could somehow help us nail the man who murdered his owner?*

Coffmann apologized to his wife, saying he'd gotten an urgent text message from the office, and he'd have to take her home and report in.

She wasn't happy that their rare date had ended abruptly but tried to put on a happy face.

"At least you took me to the movie," she said, giving him a peck on the cheek. "We finally made time for a date night. I'll have a bedtime snack for you when you get home."

As soon as he was alone, he phoned Dr. Guy Reelson, a respected local veterinarian. He was also the same animal doc who had treated Duke for his wound, which the forensics investigators had said likely was from being kicked by the perpetrator.

"You might think this is a dumb question, doc, but would Duke be able to recognize who hurt him?" Coffmann asked.

The veterinarian said nothing for a few seconds, as if thinking through carefully how to respond.

"You there, doc?" the sheriff asked.

"Not so dumb, Ethan. Not so dumb at all, the more I think about it," Reelson said. "Do you have a few seconds?"

"Go for it, doc."

"Animal psychologists have done a lot of research in recent years. They've determined that dogs are much more intelligent than we once thought."

The sheriff asked: "Like the dogs that help us find the enemy in Afghanistan, doc? And like seeing eye dogs?"

"Exactly, but even much smarter than we have ever imagined, Sheriff. It seems that dogs are invested not only with intelligence, but also with feelings, memory, emotions, reasoning.

"Dogs can read us and somehow sense what we are sensing," Reelson added. "They have an extraordinary ability to tune in to our body language, and when we get depressed, sad or sulk, or when we're hurting, our dogs sense that.

"What I'm saying is that dogs and humans are more alike, according to some experts, than they are different. Some dogs don't know they're dogs. They think they're people.

"And we know a lot more about canines than we once did. Dogs and people have a lot of things in common—their DNA and their inner organs, for example, are very similar to ours. So much of a dog's insides—their brains, heart, bladder, kidneys—are like ours.

"Go on YouTube, Sheriff. There's a clip of a dog dragging an injured dog to safety from off a busy, dangerous highway in South America. There's another clip of a dog in Texas swimming out to a struggling baby deer, grasping it by the neck with his jaws and rescuing it from drowning.

"Dogs might be smarter and braver and have better hearts than you or me," the vet said. "So, in answer to your initial question, in my professional opinion, Duke would be able to recognize who kicked him and killed his owner. How he'd react if he came in contact with the murderer, I don't know. But I predict you would see him respond accordingly."

When High Sheriff Ethan Coffmann got a beep on his phone, he quickly thanked Doc Reelson and said he'd get back to him.

"Coffmann here."

"We got a hit—a big hit, Sheriff." It was special agent Hansen.

"We've even got him on camera loading up his truck. Rough looking great big dude—arms the size of small tree trunks. He was about to leave the state, in my opinion. Asked him if we could search the premises. Said we couldn't without a search warrant. Got nervous and said we were harassing him. Threatened to call a lawyer. Got downright ugly. Demanded that we arrest him or let him go. We told 'em we have a legal right to take him in and hold him temporarily as a person of interest. Cuffed the son of a bitch. So we've got him in custody. Goes by the name of David Patrick Jackson III. And guess what?"

"Tell me," Coffman said, hardly able to contain his excitement.

"We've already been in touch with Emma Della Davis. Shown her the pictures of him and his truck—all different angles. She says he's definitely the man she remembers seeing that day at McDonald's. Even remembers, from the picture we showed her, a mole on his little chin chin. Plus, he's almost a perfect match for our forensic profile. That little gay graphic artist at your local paper got it 'bout right."

"So where is he now?"

Hansen told the sheriff the suspect was being held in the county's law enforcement interrogation room.

Coffmann knew the small, drab, soundproof room well, having used it hundreds of times to help extract confessions. It had purposely been designed and furnished, with a table and three hardback chairs, to be uncomfortable. The suspect sat in one chair. Across from the table, two interrogators sat in the other chairs. The walls were blank, except for a one-way wide mirror, with a built-in video camera and sound recorder, on one wall. That was so other investigators could watch the suspect's body language and parse every word he or she said.

"Hold him right there, guys," Coffmann said. "I'm on my way."

"Don't worry, Sheriff. This bastard ain't going anywhere."

Chapter 22
Angry Witness

The high sheriff stepped on the Crown Vic's gas pedal and activated his police siren. No time for getting stalled in traffic.

As he sped toward the police interrogation room, he put a quick call in to the county prosecutor, Daniel Boone IV. Boone, who had played a key role in sending many a criminal to state prison—and had been successful at getting the death penalty for some of the more diabolical murderers—answered on the first ring.

"What'chu up to, Ethan?" the veteran prosecutor said. "Got any bites from our little gizmos up in the sky?"

The sheriff updated him about the drone surveillance and how it had pinpointed the red pickup truck. He also briefed him quickly on how his deputies had taken "a person of interest" into custody.

"So you've made an arrest? Yippee!" the prosecutor said gleefully.

"Not yet, but we're hoping he caves under interrogation, Dan. We're going to tell him he left his DNA at the murder scenes and it's a match from DNA on the glass he drank from in the interrogation room."

"I'm guessing that's a lie but a legal one, Ethan. You're trying to get him to confess, right?"

"I realized, Dan, that we can't legally take a cheek swab of his DNA unless we arrest him. So that's the cocadoo story about getting it from his drinking glass. But it's my understanding of the law that we can lie to him—if it helps us get him to confess."

The prosecutor said that was absolutely correct. However, he expressed concern about what would happen if the suspect didn't confess. "You can only hold him for a few hours without arresting him,

Ethan. But I know you know that. So what happens if he doesn't confess?"

Coffmann, ready for that question, said, "We bring in the second murder victim's dog—Duke. He's a black lab mix that the murderer kicked before he left the scene."

The prosecutor was dumbfounded.

"Say that to me again, old man. Did I hear you right? You think Carrie Belle Powers' dog'll help you get a confession?"

"It's not as crazy as it sounds," the sheriff said. "I've done some quick research on the Internet. A professionally trained service dog has been allowed to testify in open court. It happened in Colorado when the dog was led into the courtroom by a vet to see how it'd react to a man accused of raping its owner.

"The rest, as they say, is history. The dog really went berserk. It growled and bared its front incisors and tried to attack the accused.

"Courtroom marshals had to restrain the angry canine. The judge overruled an objection from the defendant's attorney that calling the animal to the witness stand had been a sham, a trick to prick the sympathies of animal lovers on the jury."

"So what was the final verdict?" Boone asked incredulously.

The sheriff informed him that the accused, thanks in part to the dog's "testimony," had been found guilty and sentenced to 20 years in prison.

"So what the Sam Hill are we waiting for, Ethan? Have the vet bring Duke to the interrogation room. I'll be observing from behind the mirror. I just hope we're not barking up the wrong tree!"

Two hours later, David Patrick Jackson III sat across the table from High Sheriff Ethan Coffmann and FBI special agent Ron Hansen.

It was hot and stuffy in the interrogation room—just the way detectives liked it when they wanted to get a suspect to break.

"You're a convicted felon from North Carolina and you haven't reported to your probation officer in more than three months," Hansen said to the accused. "You're lucky we haven't already arrested you."

"I done my time—fair and square—and you got no right to haul me in here like some kind of criminal," Jackson shot back.

"You left your DNA at the murder scenes," Coffmann said. "It's a match for that DNA on your drinking glass that we've already refilled twice. You might as well confess. It'll go easier on you."

"You're lying!" Jackson exclaimed.

But the lawmen noticed that he had begun to squirm slightly. Beads of sweat had formed on his forehead. He kept sighing and rubbing the back of his neck with his right hand. At one point, he got up, walked around the table and pounded on the wall.

"Now let me the hell outta here!" he demanded.

Coffmann decided to play what he hoped was his trump card.

"Carrie Belle Powers, the second woman you strangled, had a black lab mix," the sheriff said. "The dog's name is Duke."

"So what if she had a damned flee-bitten dog?" Jackson replied.

"You kicked that animal really hard in its side with your right boot," Coffmann said. "We know the impression came from your boot because of our forensics analysis. In fact, you've got that very same boot on right now."

Growing more nervous, Jackson, sat down and looked down at his feet. Clasping his hands together on the table and cracking his knuckles, his eyes darted back up at the lawmen.

"So what? Everybody wears boots in this kinda' weather. And I don't know nothin' 'bout no dog named Duke."

"Bring the witness into the room," said Coffmann, staring into the one-way mirror.

The moment he trotted into the interrogation chamber, Duke became a different dog. He growled, bared his big front teeth and barked ferociously at David Patrick Jackson III. And then, the fur on his back standing up and his ears erect, Duke lunged toward the man who had hurt him. It was all that the handler could do to restrain him on a leash.

Duke, it was clear for everyone to see, wanted with every canine fiber in his body, to take a chunk of flesh out of the suspect. Foam slobber drooled from his mouth—spurred on by a special drink the vet had given him minutes earlier. Again, the dog—like an animal possessed with his reddened eyes and rigid body—lunged at Jackson. His bewildered handler dropped to the floor trying to get tighter control of him.

"Call him off!" a terrified Jackson pleaded. "I did it! I killed them three old women! Now just get control of that damned beast!"

"You're under the arrest for the murders of Hazel Eula Haynes, Gracie Spencer and Carrie Belle Powers," Coffmann said. "You have the right to remain silent. Anything you say can be used against you. You have the right to an attorney. If you cannot afford one..."

"Skip all that Miranda crap," the sheriff's target suspect declared. "Save your breath. Just get me away from that dog!"

Two of the high sheriff's deputies cuffed him and led him kicking and cussing and screaming to a cell in the jail's isolation unit.

Behind the one-way mirror, a forensics investigator emerged and informed the sheriff that he planned to take both a DNA blood sample and DNA cheek swab from the suspect. "I'm sure it'll just be a formality because you nailed this one, Sheriff."

From an adjoining room, the lawmen heard a dog. But this time the sound coming from it was more like that of a plaintive yelp. A whimper. It was Duke—grieving for his late owner.

"Sometimes a dog doesn't think he's a dog," Doc Guy Reelson had said. "And when you get right down to it, there's not much difference between them and us."

Epilogue

The Summer's Rest City Council voted unanimously to make Emma Della Davis grand marshal of the town's Christmas parade. Plus, McDonald's Corporation awarded Emma Della free burgers, fries and shakes for the rest of her life. CNN named her its Hero of the Year.

High Sheriff Ethan Coffmann served the rest of his term and chose not to run for reelection. He's now a county constable—patrolling the back roads of the most mountainous part of Taylor County, Tennessee. Duke, his adopted dog—and best friend—rides shotgun with him. Ethan works only during the day, always making it a point to be home by 5 o'clock so that he and his wife Laura can have an early dinner and quality family time.

For his cutting edge forensic sketch of the man wanted for murdering three women, Donald Mink was named the National Newspaper Association's "Graphic Artist of the Year." Soon thereafter, he landed a job as a professional sketch artist at a major metropolitan police department. He and his close friend sealed the deal—getting married in Iowa.

For its "innovative, compelling coverage of the horrific murders that rocked a southern Appalachian community," the *News-Journal* was nominated for the Pulitzer Prize for Public Service—the highest award in American journalism. The little daily paper finished second in the voting to the New York Times.

Jake Cravens, portly bombastic publisher of the *News-Journal*, sold his newspaper to an out-of-state media conglomerate—which allowed him to stay on as publisher. He was soon fired, however, for what the new ownership called "a breach of journalism ethics." Devoted but long suffering editor Dudley Lowery replaced him. Lowery would serve as publisher of the paper for only two years—transitioning to become a journalism professor at a small college in South Carolina.

Today, the newspaper in Summer's Rest touts itself as a "beacon for truth and the public's right to know."

David Patrick Jackson III pleaded guilty to three counts of first degree murder. He was sentenced to life in Tennessee's maximum security prison. Three attempts have been made on his life by his fellow inmates.

Summer's Rest, the conservative, God-fearing community in mountainous East Tennessee, continues to keep its jail, the largest government building in the city limits, filled to capacity. There's been recent talk of expanding the jail and beefing up local law enforcement because of a surge in crime—especially drug-related breakins, shootings and domestic assaults. The current sheriff recently complained to policymakers that his already-stretched department can't keep transporting mentally ill patients, who are not criminals, to psychiatric facilities.

Decades-old decaying, long-ago closed factories still stand and are one of the first things a visitor notices upon entering the west side of town. They continue to be a blight on an otherwise charming community. A sprawling Walmart, whose parking lot is always packed, is the favorite shopping venue for locals, to the detriment of downtown businesses which are struggling to stay viable. And Summer's Rest, with its numerous houses of worship and white crosses towering on mountains within view of the town, continues to be a place deeply Christian to its core.

A popular spot in the morning to grab a good cup of coffee and catch up on the news—the real news, not just the happenings printed in the town's newspaper—is McDonald's (pronounced MACK-DONNALDS by locals). Drop in there most any time and you'll find several "liars' tables." Sit at any one of them and be prepared to get an earful about the weather, who's taking what medicine, what's afflicting them, who saw what on Fox News, and last, but not least, Prez-i-dint Donald Trump, the political darling of East Tennesee.

Meet the Author

Larry C. Timbs Jr., a Vietnam-era USAF veteran, is a former professional journalist and retired journalism professor. He lives in Johnson City, Tenn.

Contact him at:
larrytimbs@gmail.com

Made in United States
North Haven, CT
11 September 2022